Phoenix hadn't come to Slater's room to cool off...

She'd come here because she was still unbearably lonely, and he was an extremely attractive man. He must see her as the hot little number she really wasn't cut out to be.

That must be why he didn't ask why she was here, because he knew she couldn't resist finding out what it would feel like to be in his arms, in his bed. She had to know what he thought.

"Aren't you going to ask me why I'm here?" she heard herself say.

"I already know." Slater's smile came slow and lazy over the angles of his face. "And I have exactly what you need."

ABOUT THE AUTHOR

This is Alice Orr's eighth Intrigue novel. The story is set in Acapulco, Mexico, where Alice has spent sun-drenched days and romance-filled nights, and in New York City where she lives.

In addition to her writing life, Alice is a literary agent, wife and mother. She also lectures nationally on writing and publishing.

You can write to Alice via E-mail at Connections at the Harlequin/Silhouette web site at: http://www.romance.net.

Books by Alice Orr

HARLEQUIN INTRIGUE

Don't miss any of our special offers. Write to us at the following address for information on our newest releases.

Harlequin Reader Service
U.S.: 3010 Walden Ave., P.O. Box 1325, Buffalo, NY 14269
Canadian: P.O. Box 609, Fort Erie, Ont. L2A 5X3

Heat of Passion
Alice Orr

Harlequin Books

TORONTO • NEW YORK • LONDON
AMSTERDAM • PARIS • SYDNEY • HAMBURG
STOCKHOLM • ATHENS • TOKYO • MILAN
MADRID • WARSAW • BUDAPEST • AUCKLAND

To my beloved husband, Jonathan,
always my romantic hero.

ISBN 0-373-22464-8

HEAT OF PASSION

Copyright © 1998 by Alice Orr

This edition published by arrangement with Harlequin Books S.A.

Printed in U.S.A.

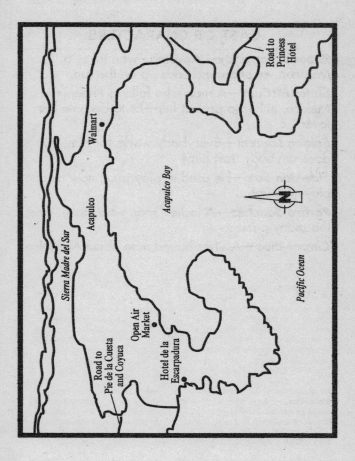

CAST OF CHARACTERS

Phoenix Farraday—A woman who takes a Mexican vacation and ends up on the run.

Slater McCain—A man who follows Phoenix to Mexico, either to protect her—or to become her lover...?

Beldon Laurent—Everybody works for him, but does anybody trust him?

SideMan Sax—He used to play jazz; now he plays it tough.

Porfiro Sanchez—A ladies' man who makes one too many passes.

Citrone Blue—A silver-haired man about Acapulco.

Prologue

Slater McCain had been undercover long enough to know the ropes. Back in the beginning he had to stay on his toes to keep track of who he was at any particular moment. These days, he hardly ever slipped up between the guy who used to be a straight cop on the job and the semisleaze he was required to become for most of his assignments. Still, "hardly ever" wasn't all the way perfect, so Slater kept watch on himself anyway, just like the character leaning against the windowsill was keeping watch on him now.

"Do I know you?" Slater asked, not bothering to keep from sounding belligerent.

"If we'd ever met before, you'd remember. You can bet on that."

Slater let the threatening tone slide over him. Undercover called for taking a certain amount of garbage from petty hoods like this one.

"You got a name?" Slater was after information first and foremost.

"SideMan's what they call me. SideMan Sax." Mr. Sax adjusted the cuffs on his too shiny suit and examined his just as shiny fingernails.

"That's a handle you don't hear every day." Slater

added with a chuckle, "Did your father pick it or your mother?"

Slater figured this dude had been christened something other than the street name that might or might not be traceable to the rap sheet he was just about a thousand percent certain to have on record in the federal investigative computer bank.

"You can leave my mother out of this." Sax added, a little more menace to his sneer.

Slater chuckled again. He always got a kick out of how punks like this one pretended to hold their mamas in such high esteem.

"I wouldn't think of causing offense," Slater said, sounding offensive anyway. "I was just making conversation."

"They call me Sax because I used to blow some horn downtown."

"You don't do that any more?"

"Nah. Now I just blow people away." He laughed at his own joke, with a dry sound that didn't have much real humor in it.

"I'll bet you blow some smoke while you're at it, too."

"You trying to say you don't believe what I'm telling you, Jack?"

Sax stepped forward as if he might be ready to make a move on Slater.

"Just blowing some smoke of my own," Slater said, easing off a little. He didn't want to play this clown too fast too soon. "So, tell me about the SideMan part. What's that stand for?"

Sax scowled at Slater a minute longer before settling back against the sill.

"Backup," he said. "I used to play backup to the headliners. I was what they call a side man."

And that's what you're still doing, Slater thought but kept it to himself this time. SideMan Sax was the kind of twisted article who hired out for somebody to keep handy like an extra piece of hardware. He'd probably do anything as long as the money was right. Slater hated anybody who carried a price tag where their conscience ought to be. He might be playing exactly that kind of bottom crawler himself on this assignment, and making a pretty convincing act of it as far as he could tell. That didn't make him one of those creeps for real, not by a long shot. At least, he hoped it didn't. Sometimes he worried that the line between acting and actually becoming the person he pretended he was could wear so thin he'd step right over it.

"So, what's your story?" Sideman was asking. He had a cocky way of bouncing his shoulders between sentences, as if he wanted to make sure everybody could see without a doubt what a tough guy from the streets they were talking to.

"Which chapter?"

Sax was obviously into doing some psyching out of his own. That meant Slater had to come across as his own kind of tough article. If his undercover act was firing on all cylinders, he'd have been figured for that as soon as he walked through the door. In fact, if Slater was playing his hand right, SideMan would bank on this bad guy act being the real McCoy. Slater's size, well over six feet and muscled out where he needed to be, was a definite advantage in creating that don't-tread-on-me impression. He intended for Sax, or anybody else who got in the way, to know that when Slater McCain decided to be uncool it would take some doing for the subduing. Slater listened to that thought and heaved a silent sigh of disgust at himself. He was getting so that even his head worked in the same tone of voice as street scum like this Sideman character.

"You listenin' to this, Mr. Laurent? This McCain guy pitches a wise answer for everything. My money says it could be the only pitch he's got, the one he makes with his mouth." SideMan sneered in Slater's direction. "My estimate is you don't need this excess baggage. Me and my two pals, Smith & Wesson, can handle whatever you got to be handled."

Slater guessed SideMan was only saying that for its one-liner value. He'd most likely be carrying something with more juice to it than an S&W. He'd be packing enough firepower to take care of just about any situation, including a guy who came across like Slater was deliberately coming across right now. "I got some muscle, too. Mine's about nine millimeters across" was the comeback Slater would have loved to spit into Sax's sneering face in a tone with enough acid in it to take the polish off his sharkskin. Slater forced himself to swallow that temptation and concentrate on his would-be employer, who had just entered the room.

Beldon Laurent gave SideMan Sax a look that cut off his snide comments like a sharp knife slicing through hot air. "Mr. McCain may be working with us," Laurent said as his short legs carried him toward the massive desk in the middle of the room. "Amiable staff relations are important to me. As long as they serve my purposes, that is. Let's try to keep it that way as long as we can, gentlemen."

Laurent eased his rounded shape into the chair behind the desk. Slater guessed there had to be a box under there to keep the guy's legs from dangling.

"I'm right about that, am I not, Mr. McCain? You do want to work for me?"

"That's what we're here to talk about, isn't it?"

"Mr. Sax's misgivings notwithstanding, why do you think I should grant this wish for you?"

"You're the one who asked me to come here. It wasn't my idea," Slater said while Sax continued to give him the cold-eyed once-over.

"This is altogether true," Laurent said with a thin, straight smile. "It is also true that you could have refused my summons, but you did not."

Speaking of cold, Beldon Laurent was the ultimate, cold like a lizard. He even looked a little lizardy with his eyes slitted up studying, first Slater, then Sax, then Slater again. Laurent tapped the tips of his fingers together, one hand to the other. His diamond pinky ring glittered in the light from the Tiffany desk lamp that probably cost a small fortune even though it didn't give off enough light to do much more than make a ring the size of Laurent's sparkle a little. Slater's research had already told him this was Laurent down to the ground. He saw something he wanted and he got it, no matter how much it might cost him.

"You put in the call. I'm here" was all Slater said.

He was supposed to act hungry. On the other hand, he wanted to be read as a potential loose cannon right from the start. That would keep Sax on guard and maybe not quite as collected as he made himself look. Slater could be something of a loose cannon when the occasion called for it and sometimes when it didn't. That hair trigger of his and the trouble it had caused him when he was above ground on the force was what made his cover as a rogue cop gone over to the wrong side of the law so believable. He had to make sure he kept the safety on that trigger, especially around the slick, slimy types that turned his stomach, types like Laurent and Sax.

"Yes, you are here." Laurent made his words clip off and drag out at the same time. "That fact tells me you are interested in my proposition—may I call you Slater? First names might put us on more congenial footing."

"That's all right with me."

According to what Slater knew about Beldon Laurent, when the cost of whatever he was after happened to include trouble or violence, he called in additional creeps like this SideMan character who didn't mind getting his hands dirty. Unfortunately, there was no concrete proof of that. Slater's assignment was to hire on as Laurent's dirty hands man of the moment. Then he was supposed to work his way as deep as he could into the Laurent operation and report back what was there.

"Slater it shall be." Laurent's lizard smile opened like a gash between cheeks pulled tight and youthful by what Slater figured to be some very expensive plastic surgery. "I prefer to do things amiably. However, I am not opposed to a hostile takeover if such is required to get the job done."

"What makes you think you'll be taking over anything?"

Slater put a strained edge on his words, making himself like the kind of guy who got tense and tense and more tense until the cork blew.

"If Mr. Laurent decides he's taking you over, you can bet he'll do it, pal," SideMan said.

Slater snapped his head around and glared as if that explosion might be close at hand. Sax sneered and chuckled in response. He'd be thinking he could play Slater like a sweet tenor without so much as breaking a sweat. If the scene was spinning out as it should, Sax would be the last person in the world to guess that Slater had some tunes of his own on the program.

"Mr. Sax is taking advantage of his insider position," Laurent said. "He is aware, after all, of the information I happen to have at my disposal about you, Mr. Mc-Cain."

"What're you talking about?" Slater asked, noticing that Laurent no longer used Slater's first name.

"I am talking about this."

Laurent tapped the file in front of him. The pale folder all but blended into the beige-and-pink veined marble of Laurent's desktop. Slater tensed visibly, as if he might be on the verge of leaping out of his seat and grabbing the file out of Laurent's hands. Slater could feel SideMan prepare himself to move on a dime if he needed to.

"What have you got there?" Slater growled.

Laurent didn't betray much reaction to Slater's show of belligerence, other than a slight glimmer in his lizard eyes. "What I have here, Mr. McCain, is a fascinating account of your more recent adventures at the hands of Lady Luck. It seems she has hardly been a faithful mistress to you."

Slater didn't say anything, and he didn't relax his posture either. He was watching Laurent now, even more closely than he'd watched Sax earlier. Unfortunately, the man wasn't anywhere near as easy to read as his hired hand.

"I don't appreciate anybody sticking their nose into my business," Slater said, shifting his stare to the file folder for a moment.

"I can certainly understand your concern. I would feel precisely the same myself." Laurent put on a silky smooth face, but Slater could still see the reptile skin underneath. "You have to understand, however, that I am a businessman. Unlike yourself, I seldom gamble on anything, not without thoroughly hedging my bets. The information I have here simply happens to be my hedge in your case.'' Laurent tapped the file folder again.

Slater settled back a bit into the pale cushioned chair. Laurent certainly had a lot of sissy colors in his office, but Slater wasn't really thinking about that now. He was too busy making himself look like a poor slob about to be whipped into submission. SideMan grinned in response to the performance.

''What are you after, and how bad do you want it?'' Slater asked Laurent.

''Badly enough to have invested in a first-class ticket from San Francisco for you already,'' Laurent answered.

''You wouldn't have gotten me to set foot back in this hellhole of a town if you didn't pay the freight.''

That was part of Slater's cover story. It also happened to be more than partly true. Slater didn't like New York City. This was where he'd been a cop, and this was where his big mouth and hot head had gotten him into trouble in the first place. He didn't have too many reasons to love the Big Apple.

''Have it your way, Mr. McCain,'' Laurent said with a nod that almost looked as if he wanted to make peace. ''Nonetheless, I actually provided the airfare because my information tells me you would not have been able to pay the freight, as you so quaintly put it, on your own.''

SideMan eased off the windowsill and edged his hand under the right side of his shiny jacket. He was obviously getting ready for how Slater might react to being so up front disrespected, but he only shrugged as if resigned to what was going on here.

''So you found out I'm broke. So what?'' was all

Slater said, letting Laurent think he'd played the odds right this time.

"Yes, that is exactly what I found out, and I have a proposition for you that could alter your financial course to a much more positive direction."

"What proposition would that be?"

"Something straight up your alley, as they say, Mr. McCain," Laurent said. "I am informed that your specialty is finding things, and those things have included people on occasion. I am further informed that you are the very best there is at this particular type of assignment."

Way to go, documents boys, Slater was thinking. The setup for his cover was working like a charm. He'd actually done enough tracking in his career that he could play the role like a champ. Still, the real finder would be his computer whiz contact in D.C.

"I know my business," Slater said, with just enough arrogance to make himself sound like the kind of cocky, macho guy Laurent would want on his team.

"I need you to find this woman."

Laurent took a second file folder from a lap drawer which he then slid back out of sight under the slab of pink-and-beige marble. He pushed the file across the polished surface toward Slater, who flipped the folder open in an obviously false casual gesture. He could all but see himself coming across as so hot for this job his Jockey shorts were steaming. A photograph of a very beautiful young woman topped the contents of the file. Slater reached to pick up the photograph to see what was underneath it, but Laurent raised his hand.

"Not just yet, Mr. McCain." The pinky diamond flashed. "I must make certain we have a working arrangement before I share anything further with you. You can understand that, can't you?''

Slater shrugged again. ''What do you want her for?'' he asked.

''Do we have a working arrangement?''

''That depends on what exactly the job is.''

''And what I am willing to pay for it?''

''That, too.''

''I am willing to pay a great deal.'' Slater guessed that Laurent was making sure to sound as if he meant every word he said. ''In return, I want you to find this young woman, as I said. Her name, by the way, is Matty Farraday. Then, Mr. McCain, once you have found her, I want you to let me know where she is.''

''Like I asked before, what do you want her for?''

''That ain't your business, buddy,'' SideMan chimed in from the windowsill.

''That's all right, Mr. Sax,'' Laurent said. ''I'm not ashamed to admit that this rather fragile-looking young woman has relieved me of a great deal of money.''

''She stole from you?''

''Yes.''

''So you want me to get your money back for you?''

''We will take care of that,'' Laurent said. ''You simply find her and then, after I have retrieved my property, I may want you to do me another service.''

''What would that be?''

''I may not mind admitting what Ms. Farraday managed to do, but I cannot allow anyone else to think they might do the same without the strongest of consequences.''

''What specific consequences would those be?'' Slater asked.

''I may want you to kill her.''

Slater felt the muscle in his cheek do a little number. He hoped it wasn't as visible as it felt. He had to look as if he were the kind of guy who didn't bat an eye at the thought of bumping off a woman, or anybody else, either. His assignment was to do whatever was necessary to work his way into Laurent's confidence. Of course, that would fall short of murder. He'd have to figure out how to avoid that requirement later on. Meanwhile, he didn't say a word. The particular word he didn't say was "No."

Chapter One

In Phoenix Farraday's opinion, the Hotel de La Escarpadura was Mexico at its best—red tile roofs, pink-washed walls, terra cotta floors, rough stone walkways—all draped in the profusion of flora and fauna that made this part of the country a wonderland for tourists from all over the world. Acapulcans were famous for their glorious gardens. They knew how to tame wildness without stifling its lush green and brilliant color in the process. That kind of tamed wildness surrounded La Escarpadura, climbed its terraces, bordered its roof and might have buried it in leaves and blossoms had skilled hands not subdued the growth.

Phoenix felt a special appreciation for this ability to trim back, tone down and keep control. She'd made a profession out of doing pretty much the same thing herself. Except she did it with people instead of with flowers. She might have called herself a gardener of the personality, but that would look a bit too strange on a business card even for her. Potential clients had enough trouble getting used to what was already printed there, or used to be, anyway.

Image Enhancement was the name she'd come up with for the business she invented for herself back in

New York City five years ago. She hired out to people who needed what she thought of as a perception make-over. They were perceived one way by the world around them when it was in their best interest, and also more accurate, for them to be perceived another. She taught her clients how to narrow the gap of that discrepancy, maybe even to eliminate it altogether, and she was good at it. She thought of herself as helping people to let the light inside them come shining through for everyone to see.

Then, she'd found herself working for Beldon Laurent. At first, she'd thought it would be an assignment like the rest. He was a reclusive businessman now interested in becoming more social, possibly even political. He was enthusiastic when she suggested philanthropy as the way into the circles he wished to enter. She'd liked that, advising Mr. Laurent on how he might use his considerable assets to do good. Then, she began to suspect that her client wasn't what he claimed to be, that the light inside him might be more dark than bright. That suspicion was the beginning of a deeper questioning for Phoenix, of the work she'd chosen to do and whether it was truly the path she should be on. She had come to Mexico to seek the answer to that for and in herself.

She'd looked up from her desk one day, back there in Manhattan, and realized that maybe she needed some image enhancement of her own. Not so much a brand-new start as a change of direction. After all, she'd worked what amounted to magic for other people in the past five years. She'd even made a silk purse out of a sow's ear, as her grandfather would have called it, on occasion. She might have kept on doing exactly that if one of those sow's ears hadn't turned out to belong to a man she'd begun to see as piggish. Just the thought of Beldon Laurent and how wrong she'd been about him made Phoenix uncomfortable. She forced her attention back to the flowers. What had she been thinking about the flowers, anyway? That's right. She was admiring those people who had the ability to subdue the natural tendency to return to jungle.

There was actually very little else, besides the disciplined gardens, that Phoenix would call subdued about La Escarpadura. At the heat of midday, of course, things quieted down to the slow-moving torpor of a sun-baked plaza, as they did throughout much of Acapulco. The rest of the time, on the other hand, especially beginning at sunset, this little cliff-side hotel was a lively place with music and laughter drifting on the breeze. When Phoenix came to the restaurant for dinner at sunset, she always asked for the same table. She was at that table tonight, facing out over the cliff onto the ocean as the sun made a silver-blue track straight toward her across the shimmering water. Tonight, just as on previous nights, the sight was so beautiful it made her eyes sting.

She wasn't always here in the restaurant at sunset. Some evenings she stayed in her room two buildings away down this same ocean side of the hotel. She'd sit in the dimming light of her terrace and listen to the waves hit the rocks at the bottom of the cliff far below. She'd breathe in the scent of the pink tumble of bougainvillea along the terrace edge until the memory of exhaust fumes in Times Square had disappeared almost entirely on the soft tropical breeze. There was peace and quiet on her terrace, something she'd found precious little of back in Manhattan.

She'd chosen La Escarpadura over the fancier tourist hotels outside of town because this had been her grandfather's favorite haunt when he lived in Acapulco back in the fifties. She'd come here in part because she needed to find out how much truth there was in the stories he'd told her about his life back then. Her grandfather was, after all, known for being one of the all-time great image enhancers when it came to his yarns about himself, and she had been his most avid audience. His Acapulco stories fed her childhood fantasies and her adolescent ones, too. Now, she wanted to know which of those fantasies had some basis in truth and which were purely figments of her grandfather's very active imagination. On those ocean-breeze-swept terrace evenings, she could see, maybe more clearly than at other times, that she'd not only come to Mexico in search of the truth about her grandfather. She'd also come here in search of herself. The first step in that quest had been to go back to using her real name.

For years, mainly because of business, she'd been calling herself Matty, as in Matilda, after her mother. In one of those silly strokes of irony, Phoenix, her true name, sounded so much like a pseudonym it put people off. Her grandfather had given her the name Phoenix when she was born. He'd said it was a hopeful name. More recently, she'd come to think of it as promising a rebirth from the life that had begun to feel false into something more authentic, more in tune with her true nature, whatever that might turn out to be. Coming here to Mexico, uprooting herself from everything familiar, was essential in her mind to discovering that authenticity, or maybe rediscovering it. Her intention was to put a renewed foot forward in this different place. That suited her reclaimed name to a T—Phoenix rising out of the ashes of the past.

Then the loneliness would set in. She'd been here for

three weeks, after all, in a place where she didn't know
a soul. Sometimes, like tonight, she even felt alone in a
crowd. A tableful of people laughed and joked only a
few feet away in La Escarpadura's open air dining room,
but those few feet suddenly felt to Phoenix like the distance across the universe. The sound of their laughter
echoed around her, closing her more deeply into her iso-
lation. She could hardly have been more relieved when
a voice broke through her separateness. She looked up
eagerly before she'd had time to put up her usual guard
against strange men.

"*Señorita,* may I be so bold as to invite you for a
dance?"

She'd seen him in here before. He was dark and handsome in a slick sort of way that didn't really appeal to
her. The dark waves of his hair were streaked with silver
sheen, and his wide smile shone white against the bur-
nished bronze of his skin. He usually sat on a stool at
the far end of the bar on the opposite side of the restaurant near the archway into the courtyard. She'd seen him
watching her many times. He'd even tried to talk to her,
and once she'd thought she saw him following her from
the restaurant toward her room.

"No, thank you," she said, turning her former eager-
ness instantly cool.

"I dislike to see a lovely lady like yourself sitting so
all alone on a beautiful night like this." His voice was
slippery smooth. Phoenix could picture him using this
same tone every time he wanted to bring a woman under
the spell of his charm. The sound of it was having the
directly opposite effect on her.

"I've told you before that I don't want company,"
she said, letting her exasperation be heard.

Being a woman alone in Mexico took some getting

used to, even for Phoenix. Back in New York City she wouldn't have thought anything of stopping at a street café on her own for supper or a glass of wine. Sometimes she'd have a book with her or a magazine, but other evenings she might simply sit by herself and watch the people passing by. She'd get looks from men, of course. Occasionally, one of them might come right up and start talking to her. All she had to do then was give him a quick brush-off line like, "I'd really rather be by myself just now," and he'd go away. Acapulco wasn't quite like that. The men here weren't so easy to discourage. Phoenix taught herself to say "I'd really rather be by myself" in Spanish, but it didn't do much good. Most Acapulco gentlemen, who usually spoke English anyway, turned that response into an opportunity to comment on her being *una americana* and praise her adorable accent. She either had to be firm with them or leave. She wasn't about to leave tonight. The prospect of returning to her room, even to her lovely terrace in the moonlight, appealed to her even less than this man's unwelcome attentions.

"*Señorita,* I have heard you say that you want to be alone, but the sadness of your eyes tells me that is not true."

His own eyes were dark and flashing down at her. She stared straight and hard back into them.

"What are my eyes telling you now?"

She'd said that as coldly as she could manage, but instead of being put off he took a step closer.

"I see *tu corazón, mi señorita,*" he crooned. "Your heart is telling me you want me to sit down here with you and speak what is in *mi corazón* for you."

He grasped the back of the chair next to hers and began to slide it away from the table.

"My name is Porfiro, and I already know who you are."

"Do not sit down," Phoenix said firmly as she clutched her napkin, making a fist in her lap. She was ready to stand up and cause a scene if he persisted further.

"Now, *señorita*," he answered more syrupy than ever. "You know you don't mean that."

"I think she does."

The man's words were anything but syrupy. His tone was more reminiscent of the rough bark of the tree that sweet sap originated from. He'd come up fast behind Porfiro to tower over him by at least half a foot. Phoenix hadn't seen this man in here before. She was sure she'd remember him if she had. His size was what struck her first, imposing on her consciousness the same way he imposed upon the room. The top of his head would barely clear the archway at the restaurant entrance. His shoulders were broad as well. He was lean and spare. She could imagine his skin close to the bone and muscle all over, taut and strong. His face was handsome but wary, with skepticism etched into every line, especially those around his dark—or could they be green?—eyes. His hair was black and thick, brushed back on the sides probably to tame its unruliness. His stance and profile reminded Phoenix of ancient Aztec warrior images carved in stone.

Porfiro turned toward the craggy voice. "Do I know you, *señor*?"

"Slater McCain's the name. No, you don't know me, and I'd just as soon keep it that way. What I heard from over there at the bar gives me the feeling this young lady may feel the same."

Porfiro didn't move. A single step forward would put

him smack up against the wall of Mr. McCain's chest. The only way around that barrier would be to sidestep in obvious retreat. From what Phoenix had observed of the Mexican male ego, that would be a very difficult move for Porfiro to make even to escape a mountain of a man like this Slater McCain, especially since the laughter had faded away at the nearby table while everyone turned to watch the drama unfolding around Phoenix. She wondered if Porfiro might go so far as to start a fistfight to save face. She was about to stand up and intervene before any such violence could begin when McCain stepped backward a rangy pace giving Porfiro plenty of room to pass.

"Let's you and me talk about this another time, just the two of us, *hombre a hombre,*" McCain said in a tone with less challenge to it than before.

Phoenix could see that he was giving Porfiro a way to salvage his ego in front of this roomful of people. Porfiro rocked back with a hand on one hip in a self-assured pose that made less pointed the distance he had to stare upward to meet McCain's eyes. Both men held that stance for a long moment while Phoenix held her breath.

"*Sí, mi amigo,*" Porfiro said at last. "*Hombre a hombre.*"

Phoenix breathed more easily then. She half expected them to clasp hands in an internationally recognized symbol of masculine solidarity, but apparently neither man wanted to carry their truce that far. Porfiro let go of the chair, and McCain took another step backward. Porfiro nodded once and turned sharply from the table. Still, he didn't leave immediately. He looked back at Phoenix one more time.

"I will see you again, *señorita*," he said, his wide smile restored.

He walked away then. Phoenix couldn't help chuckling to herself as she watched his back recede, military straight, through the archway that led from the restaurant to the courtyard and the exit from the hotel grounds. When he was out of sight at last, she breathed a sigh of relief.

"Some men find it hard to take no for an answer." Slater McCain's voice had lost some of its cragginess.

Phoenix looked up at him, craning her neck as Porfiro had so obviously not wanted to do.

"That's true," she said.

She was trembling a little, and she knew that wasn't happening solely because of the tense scene Mr. McCain had just now so ably defused. His presence added an extra pulse of heat to the tropical night for her. He was a very attractive man with hair and eyes as dark as Porfiro's. Otherwise, McCain impressed her as being as earthy solid as Porfiro was slick and artful.

"If you're all right now," McCain said, "I'll leave you to enjoy your meal in peace."

"Don't go."

Phoenix responded so quickly she didn't have time to realize she was going to say that. She took a breath to compose herself. What she had here tonight was not peace but solitariness. Suddenly, she felt as if she'd always been alone, with never many friends and no family to speak of since her grandparents died. She'd worked so hard building up her business there'd been little time for friends or anything else particularly personal. That was one of the things she hoped to change, a major way she intended the new Phoenix here in Mexico to be different from the old Matty back in New York. She'd tried to make at least one connection here, with her grandfather's former sidekick, Citrone Blue. He turned out to be out of town and no one knew when he'd be back so she'd ended up alone again. Most of the time her solitude didn't really bother her, but tonight wasn't one of those times. Otherwise, she'd be back on her terrace right now instead of gazing up at Slater McCain.

Her heart tripped faster just looking at him, and she could feel her breath rising high and shallow in her throat. Her still rational mind comprehended that she hadn't been with a man for a very long time. This, combined with her protracted solitariness and restless mood, made for a potentially powerful brew. She should consider her reaction to this man in light of that heady mix. She shouldn't let her good judgment be jeopardized by what was most likely a momentary aberration of her senses. She'd be foolish to do that.

Warm laughter rippled from the surrounding tables once more. Phoenix could pick out phrases of companionable talk in English, Spanish and even German. The brilliant blooms just outside the open window wall next to her table began to release their perfume most provocatively at this hour. Her glass of mineral water sat unsipped and sweating moisture on the table in front of her. In that instant, it dawned on Phoenix that the last thing she wanted on this particular evening was to sip at anything. Mineral water and surrounding voices would not be enough to satisfy her tonight. She could feel herself filling up, like a fiesta balloon, her restlessness roaring more loudly through her veins by the moment.

"Won't you sit down and let me buy you a drink?" she said to Slater McCain. "That's the least I can do to thank you for such a dramatic rescue."

He gazed down at her. For a breathless second, Phoenix wondered what she would do if he brushed her off as she'd done so many times to so many men in response to approaches not much different from this one. Then, he smiled. That smile ended far short of the breadth Porfiro would have managed. Still, the change in Slater's expression all but took her breath away once more. The curving of his lips emphasized the hollows beneath his cheekbones and deepened his dark eyes into shadow in the flickering light from the white candle inside the glass hurricane lamp on the table.

"I'll get the drinks," he said. "What'll you have?"

Phoenix was about to ask for mineral water as usual when another impulsive response leapt from her lips.

"I'll have a *margarita*," she said, then couldn't help but add, "easy on the *tequila*, please."

She might call herself Phoenix Farraday, but part of her was still Matty after all.

Chapter Two

In a way she was what Slater expected, and in a way she wasn't. First of all, she was even more beautiful in person than in the photograph he'd seen back in Beldon Laurent's office. Looking into those big blue eyes of hers, Slater had no doubt she could con an Eskimo out of his mittens. She was a spellbinder for sure, and that kind of talent came in very handy to a thief. Too bad she'd misjudged how far her looks and charm could get her when she took up with guys as evil as Beldon Laurent and SideMan Sax. Slater told himself he didn't feel sorry for her for doing that. All that sweetness of hers had to be mostly an act. He thought maybe some of it was sincere. He could tell she really didn't like being hit on by slippery types like that character back at her table. Speaking of whom, who was he, anyway? Slater believed in checking out everybody who got in his way. The bartender had just taken Slater's order when he slipped a hundred-*peso* note across the highly polished surface.

"What's the story on the *hombre* I was talking to just now?"

Slater motioned toward the table on the other side of the restaurant. He figured the bartender had been keeping a close eye on what happened back there just in case it escalated into a shoving match. The bartender slipped his palm over the cash then peeked at it between his fingers, probably checking out the amount before deciding how much he would tell.

"Name's Porfiro Sanchez," the bartender said. "He comes in here sometimes, mostly to check out the women or maybe to pick up a drive-around job from the *turistas*."

"He's a tour guide?"

"*Sí*. Drives a big, black car for one of the outfits down on the Costera."

Slater had examined the Acapulco map on his way here and recognized the name of the main drag, La Costera Miguel Aleman, through the center of town.

"You wouldn't know the name of that outfit, would you?" he asked.

"I couldn't tell you that."

Slater understood that might mean the bartender knew the answer but wasn't giving it up.

"What can you tell me?"

The man swept the already immaculate surface of the bar with a white rag before responding. "Sanchez hangs out at one of the big hotels out on the strip by the airport. Does tours out of there in the mornings, sometimes afternoons when it's not too hot for you *gringos* to take."

"Which big hotel would that be?" Slater slipped a twenty-*peso* note across the bar this time.

The bartender palmed the note and slipped it into his pocket. "I think maybe the Princess."

"Thanks," Slater said as the bartender went off to get the drinks Slater had ordered.

Slater knew maybe he didn't need to spend that much cash to find out about some stud making passes, but it was Laurent's expense account money, so why not? What Slater really wanted to know about was Matty Farraday or Phoenix or whatever she was calling herself now. He figured he'd tapped this bartender enough for one night. Besides, Slater had made contact with the woman. He could pick up what he needed to know firsthand. And he'd already done enough research to come here with a picture of what to expect of her in his mind.

Slater liked to know the territory he was scouting in advance. He didn't care for surprises. He researched the scene up front so any situation he walked into was already half-familiar to him. In ninety-nine percent of the cases he handled, Slater could figure a person out from top to bottom ahead of time, like putting a puzzle together. People are predictable, even criminals. Slater was good at psyching out their patterns, and he didn't intend to let a little bit of a thing like Miss Matty Phoenix whatever screw with his system.

Of course, she wouldn't be considered a little bit of a thing by most measures. She was five seven or so. Still, next to him, she seemed pint-size. She had a fair amount of flesh on her bones though, and all in the right places. Those places and how good they looked had registered somewhere below his belt buckle as soon as he saw her sitting there with that Mexican blouse pulled down just far enough and the outline of her breasts visible under the white cloth. Slater put those dangerous thoughts out of his head right then and told them to stay out. She was a wrongo, a thief, whether she was stealing from another wrongo or not. A thief was forever on the other side of the fence from the solid citizens of the world as far as Slater was concerned.

It was a code of honor for him never to cross that fence in a personal way. Other guys on the force might get involved with women they collared, but not Slater. Especially off-limits were the ones who auctioned off their honesty for money. That's what this woman had done. She'd seen a chance to put her hands on her boss's cash, and she'd done it. Then she'd skipped out of the country. She'd even changed her name, or at least part of it. Only criminals did that. She'd run to Mexico with its long history of harboring outlaws and never asking question number one about why they were on the lam. She'd known enough to choose an out-of-the-way hotel, too. She was smart all right, just not smart enough to keep a pro like Slater from finding her.

All the way down here from New York, he'd studied her photograph. He couldn't stop studying it. Those big, blue eyes had intelligence behind them. She operated her own business, which required brains, even if she used them for making a creep like Beldon Laurent look good to the world. Image Enhancement she called it, which amounted to whitewashing the blackhearted in Slater's estimation. Still, it took some savvy to be good at what she did, and, according to the information he'd come up with about her, she was good at it. She'd also managed to steal from Laurent who was no mental midget himself. She had to be pretty smart to manage that, though maybe not so wise. Crossing a man like Laurent was about as smart as stepping on a rattlesnake at high noon.

Slater looked back toward where she was sitting and was surprised to see her walking across the restaurant toward him. He couldn't help indulging himself in a fantasy of how it would be to pull that Mexican blouse off all the way. She was only a couple of feet away when that fantasy made him smile the kind of smile a woman is probably looking for when she comes strutting straight up to a man in a café like this one. He was waiting for her to flash him a matching smile in return when she did something that didn't fit the pattern he had her plugged into. He was looking right into her blue eyes when it happened. He couldn't have misread what he saw, and what he saw was fear. In fact, if he hadn't reached out and grabbed her arm, he'd bet a lot of *pesos* she'd have run away.

"Hey, what's the matter?" he asked. "I thought we were going to have a drink and get to know each other a little bit."

"Please," she said, resisting his grip without making a scene of it.

She sounded scared, too, but her job was showing people how to act like something they really weren't. Maybe she was doing that herself now.

"Please," she said again. "I made a mistake. I don't think this is a good idea."

So that was going to be her dodge. The old hard-to-get routine.

"You'd rather be by yourself on a beautiful night like this? Is that what you're telling me?"

She stared him straight in the eyes for a moment.

"No," she said. "I'm lonely, and the last thing I want to be is alone."

He hadn't expected that. Maybe she was shrewd enough to figure this for the kind of situation where truth is the best gambit.

"Then why are you leaving?"

She couldn't hold the stare any longer. She took a deep breath and looked down at the floor.

"I just think it's the smart thing to do."

She was really good at this. She actually sounded awkward.

"Look," she said. "I'm grateful to you for getting rid

of Porfiro what's his name, but I really have to get back to my room now.''

She tugged against his grip. He'd pretty much forgotten he was still holding on to her. She glanced up at him long enough for him to see that her cheeks were flaming red, and not just from too much sun. Could she fake a blush like that? Slater didn't think so. He let go of her arm.

''Sorry,'' he said. ''I didn't mean to clamp on to you like that.''

''You're not the one who needs to apologize. You helped me out and now I'm giving you the brush-off. It's just that I don't do this kind of thing, if you know what I mean.''

''That's okay. I understand,'' he said and told himself he wasn't actually falling under her spell. He stood up from the bar stool anyway, remembering that maybe he should act like a gentleman whether he thought she was a lady or not. ''Please, sit down,'' he said indicating the next stool.

Sometimes when women gazed up at him and had to strain their necks to do it, as she was now, he felt like a too-tall freak who needed to be shrunk back to normal size. She didn't make him feel that way. She gazed up at him as if she were taking him in, the way she might take in a statue or a mountainside, because she liked the look of it.

''Come on, sit down,'' he repeated. ''You'll get a charley horse in your neck if you don't.''

She smiled, and the lights came on in her eyes. That, plus the high color in her cheeks which were dusted by a scattering of pale freckles, made her even more dazzling. In that instant, Slater knew he'd have to work at keeping his head together around her.

"Let's just have that one drink we were talking about. I've already ordered it," he said.

He'd pulled the stool away from the bar for her to sit down. She looked at the stool then back at him. She was either sincerely reluctant or the best actress he'd ever met. He smiled down at her. Some women had told him he had his own brand of dazzle. He did his best to put whatever that might be into his smile. Maybe it worked because she actually did sit down, though on the very edge of the stool as if to be prepared for a fast takeoff.

"Why'd you do it this time?" he asked.

She looked at him as if she hadn't a clue what he was talking about.

"You said you never do this kind of thing," he explained. "I assume you meant you don't usually ask men you don't know to have drinks with you. What made you do it this time?"

She stared directly into his eyes, the same way she had before. He had the feeling she was deciding whether he merited more truth, or if she cared enough to bother telling it.

"I told you. I was feeling lonely," she said.

Her eyes drew him in when she said that, so much so he heard himself nattering, "A woman like you? Lonely?"

He could hardly believe he'd come out with such a drugstore variety line. He sounded like a jerk, trying to palm himself off as a pickup artist.

"You know what I mean," he added and wondered if his cheeks might be red, too, now. He was certainly blushing inside.

She laughed a full, rich laugh that tinkled down his spine from one vertebra to the next.

"I know what you mean," she agreed. "Nobody ever

admits to being lonely because it's so uncool to be thought of that way, as if it makes you a real loser to be by yourself. Actually, I came to Mexico to be just that. Then all of a sudden tonight I found I was tired of my own company. You happened to come along just after I made that discovery.'' She dropped her eyes.

Winsome, she definitely was that.

"So you traveled all the way to Acapulco to be by yourself?"

"Among other things."

"What other things?"

The minute he said that, he knew it was a mistake. He'd pushed too hard, and now she'd probably run off. Instead, she answered him.

"I came here to be in the place my grandfather used to tell me stories about."

Well, it was an answer anyway. What had he expected? For her to blurt out that she ripped off her boss and came here as a getaway?

"Your grandfather was from Mexico?"

"No, but he lived here for a while, right in this hotel, back in the fifties."

"I saw the sign out front," he said. "This place was pretty hot back then."

"Yes, it was."

The sign on the front veranda said that La Escarpadura had been a favorite hangout for a lot of Hollywood types back then. Movie stars came down here to get away from the limelight. And maybe from the law, too, Slater thought. He looked around at the colorful decor, the view from atop a high cliff over the ocean. The place had a lot of character. He could imagine some pretty wild parties going on here back in the old days.

"Your grandfather hung out with that Hollywood crowd?"

"So he used to tell me when he was alive."

The guitar and keyboard combo had come off their break and were beginning to play. The tune they struck up first was "My Way." Slater would have expected something a little more native. He looked at Phoenix. He saw the laughter in her eyes, and he couldn't help but laugh himself.

"I guess they're honoring yet another Hollywood gang," she said.

Slater stared. He hadn't a clue what she might be talking about.

"You know," she said. "Frank Sinatra and the Rat Pack."

"Right. Right."

"Bad joke. I apologize again."

"No, not a bad joke. Maybe I just don't have a sense of humor tonight."

"That's not the way it works. The joker has to make the jokee laugh. That's the first rule of joke telling."

"I see."

Slater nodded his head, the same one he'd vowed to watch around this woman. Except that, when he'd made that pledge to himself he had no idea she'd turn out to be so likable. He had to remember what he was here for.

"Here are our drinks," he said as the bartender set the frosty glasses in front of them.

She moved even closer to the edge of her stool, as if the spell of the laugh they'd shared had just been broken and she was about to run away after all.

"Oh, come on," he urged. "Just one drink, in honor of all Hollywood gangs past, present and future."

She sighed and settled back a little. "All right, just

one. You did tell him to make it light on the *tequila,* didn't you?''

Slater stared into her blue eyes and felt a little awkward himself for a moment. He'd had his reasons for coming to the bar to order the drinks. He'd wanted to do so out of her hearing. That way he could ask for one heavy on the alcohol for her. She'd be more forthcoming with the information he needed if she was a bit liquored up, and with all that lime taste in a *margarita* she wouldn't be likely to notice the difference. He looked at her now in the soft, peach-colored lighting that was intended to be flattering. He couldn't help thinking she'd be beautiful even under the starkest of fluorescents. She gazed back at him with a small, tentative, even dreamy smile on her lips, and he found himself wishing he knew the content of those dreams.

Slater turned reluctantly away from her smile and called to the bartender. "Hey, *amigo,* I made a mistake on that drink order. Make one of those very, very light on the *tequila.*"

Chapter Three

"Whaddaya want?"

Phoenix stepped back from the closed door at the sound of the harshness in Slater's voice. She'd felt a tension under his charming exterior back in the restaurant before she'd gone to her room, supposedly for the rest of the night. She'd sensed there was another, not quite so charming side to him even then, but this impatient bark through his hotel room door was much farther down that darker side than she'd expected.

"It's Phoenix," she answered, well aware that if she had a brain in her head she'd make a run for it instead.

There was silence from behind the door. Maybe he wasn't as interested in her as she'd thought. When he took his room key out of his pocket and left it on the bar long enough for her to be sure to see the number on the tag, she'd assumed he was passing on information for possible future use. Maybe he hadn't intended any such thing. Maybe she should take her own good advice and get out of here right now. She was about to do just that when the door opened, first a crack, then wider, until he was standing full in the doorway leaning against the frame. He was even taller than she remembered him to be, or maybe she was just feeling suddenly small.

The night had been sultry as she walked over here from her room. Now it was sultrier still. She understood that he was the reason for the rising steaminess she couldn't ignore. She couldn't breathe easily because of it. He'd made her a bit breathless back in the restaurant, but this was much worse. The size of him took up too much of everything around him, including the air. Or, maybe it was the way his green eyes, dark now in the shadow of the doorway, seemed to pull the night into their depths that made her feel almost giddy. She couldn't help wanting to see into those deep regions, all the way to the bottom of them, though she suspected that their secrets might frighten her.

"Come in," he said in a voice as deep and almost as mysterious as his eyes.

Phoenix would have liked to say she hesitated, but she didn't. She nodded a thank you and stepped over the threshold.

"I hope it's not too hot for you," he said.

Phoenix almost jumped out of her skin, as if he might have heard her thoughts about how sultry he made her feel.

"I don't like air-conditioning," he continued. "I prefer real air to the canned kind."

"Oh, yes," she said. "I feel the same way."

She wasn't sure why she said that. She could use a blast from a truly frigid air-conditioning unit right now if only to cool her blood some. But then, she hadn't come here to cool off, had she? She'd come here because, even after their talk in the bar and the laughter they'd shared, she was still unbearably lonely, and he was an extremely attractive man. Of course, she couldn't give that as an answer when he asked why she was here as he was bound to do.

"Can I get you a drink?" he asked.

"No, thank you."

"Are you sure? You're looking a little flushed."

Her hand flew to her cheek. She was warm, and maybe flaming red as well, even in this subdued light from the one light he had on by the bed. She really was embarrassed now. He must see her as the hot little number she really wasn't cut out to be. That must be why he didn't ask why she was here, because he knew she couldn't resist finding out what it would feel like to be in his arms, in his bed. She had to know if that was what he thought.

"Aren't you going to ask me why I came to your room?" she heard herself say.

"I already know."

He'd walked to the dresser and picked up one of the glasses that was sitting there on a tray next to a bottle of water and another bottle that looked like it might be liquor. He turned back toward her. His smile came slow and lazy over the angles of his face. The sensuousness of that smile simmered across the room toward her. Of course, he knew why she was here.

"You needed ice," he said.

"What?" His answer was so unexpected that she blurted her response.

"You were all out of ice in your room, and you figured I might just have some, so here you are. You were right about that, too. I do have ice." He lifted the top off the ice bucket on the tray behind the bottles. "I have exactly what you need."

His voice dropped even lower on those final words and thrilled through her like the thrum of a very deep and vibrant guitar chord. She shuddered, and she could feel her breath go shallower still. This man, the sultry night, the scent of flowers on a soft breeze through the open doors onto his terrace. The spell of all that was more than she could stand. She could feel herself about to be swept up on that breeze and carried out beyond the terrace rail over the expanse of the perilous, bottomless sea. This is what she'd come here for, of course, to be precisely that carried away. Now, the prospect terrified her. She swallowed to cover her fear and to urge her breath toward a more normal rhythm if that were any longer possible.

"Water or whiskey or both?" he asked with the ice bucket top still in his hand and his dark eyes drawing her in just as they'd drawn in the night a few moments ago.

"Water," she managed to reply.

"And ice," he stated, as if to confirm his explanation of why she'd shown up at a strange man's door late at night.

"Yes, ice."

She'd wanted only to nod, but speaking the words made her feel more in control no matter how far that might be from the reality of her current state of being. He took a pair of tongs from the bucket and picked up a cube of ice. The cube dropped into the glass, then was followed by another. The clink of one cube hitting the next resounded in her soul like the sealing of her fate, but she made no move to escape. Instead, she longed to snatch the ice-filled glass from his hand and press it to her flaming cheek. She wondered if her skin might sizzle audibly when she did that. She noted how this idle wondering drifted across her mind like vapor. Her thoughts were turning as languid as the night. Her limbs felt limpid and drifting, too. She might have blamed the *tequila,* except that she'd left her *margarita* hardly tasted on the bar before leaving there.

"Let's sit outside," he said.

He had a glass in each hand, one filled with clear liquid, the other with brown. He motioned toward the open doors. Phoenix stared up at him for a moment. She hadn't expected him to take his time this way, make them drinks, sit on the terrace, chat for a while. She'd thought he would grab her as soon as she walked in the door. She'd been a little afraid of that happening. Maybe she'd hoped for it, too, for everything to happen so unstoppably fast that she wouldn't have to hold herself responsible for it later. This gradual approach of his was giving her too much time to think. She didn't want that.

Still, the slowness was also like the place and the night, seductive and luring her in. She walked ahead of him out onto the terrace and sat down on the wicker divan which was identical to her own, back on her own terrace to her own room. Everything sensible about her said that back there was where she ought to be right now as he sat down next to her. His size took up so much of the width of the divan that his thigh touched hers. She could feel the heat of him through her cotton skirt. She edged slightly away.

"This isn't your cup of tea, is it?" he said.

"What do you mean?"

Her tormented emotions had her so confused she thought for a moment he might be referring to the drinks he still held in his hands.

"Coming to a man's room like this," he said. "I get the feeling it's not the usual thing you do."

Phoenix took a deep breath then plunged. "Maybe I want it to be," she said. "At least, for tonight."

He looked at her and kept very still for a long moment. The moon shone low over the bay in place of the sun which had set so beautifully earlier. The moonlight was brilliant against the black, star-pricked heavens. A path of silver-white shimmered across the dark water toward the terrace where Phoenix and Slater sat. They were up so high on the edge of the cliff that no land was visible below them, only sea and sky. They might have stepped over the balcony onto that moonpath and walked the water like a god and goddess. She could feel that kind of power crackling in the scented air around them.

Slater turned away from her to put the glasses down on the wicker table next to the divan. In that instant, she felt the absense of his gaze like a chill across her face from the cold center of the moon. Phoenix shivered, but when he turned back toward her she was instantly warm all over again. She couldn't help smiling at the strangeness of those two sensations coming so close together, one upon the other. She was still smiling when his lips touched hers.

The magnetic force of his dark emerald eyes had been powerful, but that was nothing compared to the compulsion with which the breath of his kiss drank her in. She couldn't have moved her mouth away from his if she wanted to, and she didn't want to. She smiled more widely at the sheer, pulsing joy he was pulling her into. Her eyes were still slightly opened, but the moonlight had disappeared. The breadth of Slater's shoulders blocked out the moon, the ocean, everything, and she didn't care. She would have liked him to blot out all of life for her, if only for tonight.

His tongue had found the place where her smile parted her lips and pressed between them into her mouth. She felt the intimacy of that invasion in a thrust of sensation that sought its mark between her thighs and spread there with a sudden, undeniable warmth. She could all but scent her own desire mingling with the aroma of blossoms on the tropical air. With all that was womanly in her, she wanted more than anything in that moment for him to catch that essence of her, too, and breathe it in. She pressed her mouth even more inseparably to his and met his tongue with her own.

She'd never kissed a man so hungrily before. She circled his tongue with the tip of hers, voraciously, as if from an appetite that must be fulfilled or she might die from longing for it. She sucked at him and moaned deep in her throat as she did. She wanted to bring him inside of her, now his tongue, later the rest of him. She reached her hands up into the darkness of his hair and the surprising coolness of the waves of it around her fingers. That was the only coolness she felt from either of them as his moan answered hers and he dragged her to him, close and hard. She wasn't startled by that sudden roughness. It was what she wanted, at least she thought she did, inasmuch as she could manage to think at the moment.

She wrenched aside any shred of doubt that might still be plaguing her and breathed one word against his lips. "Yes," she said on a moan that he must feel as much as hear. "Yes."

He groaned and lifted her to pull her over on top of him. She gasped. She could feel the hardness of him against her as she was certain he meant her to do. Her first instinct was to grind herself against him, to pound her body into his, like the waves pounding the rocks at the bottom of the cliff below them. She doubted she had the willpower to hold herself back from doing that, but somehow she did.

Phoenix felt the pulses of the breeze in her blood. Her

hips longed to move in an undulating dance against the hardness between his thighs. He groaned again, and she could hear longing identical to her own in the sound. She was torturing him with her closeness, the same way he was torturing her. Just by moving her hips in a sinuous flow and rubbing her breasts against his chest, she would be able to make this mountain of a man do anything she wanted him to do. That was a power she had never before realized she possessed. She moved and he moaned yet again, more agonizingly than ever.

He clamped her more tightly to him so suddenly she had no time to prepare for the thrust of desire that rocketed through her. She'd been a fool. He was the one in power here. She knew that to be undeniably true at the same instant he reached down and began to pull up her skirt. The implication of that movement and what it must inevitably lead to startled Phoenix into stillness for the moment. The long folds of her skirt whispered against her skin as he dragged them upward. She wished for one last tantalizing instant that she was the kind of woman she had come here to be. Only disappointment accompanied her recognition that she was not. Her hand shot out and covered his before it could move an inch farther.

"Stop," she said, shocked by the sound of her voice nearly strangling with what felt like tears. "I can't."

Before he could respond, Phoenix had torn herself from his arms and was running as fast as she could through his terrace door, out of his room, away from temptation stronger than any she had ever known.

Chapter Four

Slater woke up hot and disgruntled. He was on top of the wrinkled bedspread with a pillow stuffed under his head, and he was alone. He'd been alone when he threw himself down here last night after pacing savagely back and forth across his floor and terrace for so long that he was surprised not to find a path worn in the tiles by the time he was done. He'd tossed restlessly through the night, shaking himself awake over and over again until the dawn began to pale the darkness. He'd slept a while then, a shallow slumber through which he reached for her repeatedly and she just as repeatedly melted away before he could so much as touch her soft, fragrant skin. That fragrance from twilight sleep mingled with the breeze from his terrace as Slater came finally fully awake with the sun sparkling brightly through his terrace doors and the gulls shrieking what sounded to him like, "Fool, fool, fool," as they swooped through the air beyond the terrace railing.

He was a fool all right, a bigger one than he'd ever allowed himself to be in his life. Slater grabbed the pillow from beneath his head and threw it between the open doors so hard it hit the bougainvillea hanging over his balcony and sent dislodged blossoms tumbling to the terrace floor. He swore under his breath and ran his fingers through his hair. He felt like bashing his head against the stucco wall. Maybe he could knock some sense into himself that way. Last night, he'd made one of the stupidest moves of his career. He'd let an assignment get out of control because *he* got out of control.

According to Slater's personal code, control was one thing he must absolutely never lose. He had learned the hard way what could happen when he didn't follow that rule. He'd almost washed himself out of the police work he loved. His temper did that to him. Now he was discovering other parts of himself that could be just as dangerous, and this was a new experience for him. He'd never had a woman get to him the way this one did last night. Fortunately, what happened between them hadn't gone completely over the top, but he could take no credit for that.

The danger wasn't just about sex, either. Sex could work in a cop's favor sometimes. In fact, he knew about lots of cases where the bed had been a principal weapon in getting the job done. Slater, on the other hand, didn't do that, at least he never had before. Using sex to collar a perp was one of the things he'd told himself he would never do. *Too sleazy for me,* he'd always said. There were names for somebody who did that kind of thing. As he saw it, those names applied whether you were a man or a woman, but last night had been different. What happened between Phoenix and him had nothing to do with why he was in Mexico.

He could hardly believe the way he'd behaved. She'd come close to him, and he was lost. He couldn't be certain exactly when it happened, maybe the first minute he opened the door and saw her standing there looking scared to death. From then on, he was a goner. If she hadn't called a halt when she did, he'd have been guilty of more than just misjudgment. He'd have been the perpetrator of a professional disaster.

Slater cursed under his breath some more as he stood and stretched as best he could without scraping his knuckles on the rough plaster of the ceiling. He was stiff from sleeping so fitfully with his long legs at odd angles across the bed. He would have liked to go for a run. He'd take off down the winding road that led from the hotel to the town. He'd find the steepest way back up the hillside and push himself to keep running all the way until his lungs felt as if they were about to explode. Maybe he could blast her out of his system that way, but he didn't have time for a run right now.

Slater had to concentrate on damage control. Unfortunately, all he could think about was Phoenix Farraday. His original plan was to establish a rapport with the subject. He shook his head and sighed as he stretched again and cranked his neck to loosen the tight muscle he could feel there. He'd established rapport all right, but not the kind that got the job done. What he'd allowed to happen last night was the kind of situation that could screw a job up so bad there'd be no chance of unscrewing it again. What happened last night was that he'd allowed himself to care, and this was the biggest no-no of all.

When Slater was on a case, he made certain to have himself ready for whatever might arise. Otherwise, he could get himself killed. He hadn't been ready for last night because nothing like that had ever crossed his path before, nothing like Phoenix, either. She'd blindsided him in a way he wouldn't have thought possible before it happened. She'd made him forget who he was, and who she was, too. Ever since New York, he'd been wondering how he'd get around telling Laurent he'd found her once he did. Slater wasn't about to be the cause of getting a woman killed, whether she was a thief or not. He'd always known there was no chance he'd turn her over to a creep like Laurent and, of course, no chance Slater would harm her himself. In fact, after last night, all he could think about was how he could protect her. That's the power of the effect she had on him, a power that was not to be denied.

Slater unbuttoned his shirt and was pulling it off when he stopped to wonder if she could have known what she was doing all along. She could have come here to his room deliberately to draw him under her spell. She wouldn't be the first woman to pull that on a guy. She was a thief, after all. Maybe she was some other things, too. He remembered her face, as if he could ever forget it, the liquid of her eyes shining in the moonlight almost as if they were filled with tears. Every cop instinct he possessed told him she hadn't been faking that any more than he could have faked what he felt when he looked into those eyes.

Or maybe he just wanted to believe that. What guy wanted to think a woman was gazing up at him and moaning in his arms because she was trying to get something out of him? The memory of Phoenix's shining eyes and the sweet sounds she'd made last night brought other memories, and sensations, too. He thought he caught the smell of her hair on the breeze that blew through the open doors onto the terrace. Slater shoved those doors shut with a bang as if to shut the thought of her outside, but it didn't work. He'd just met her, and she was under his skin already. He had to get her out before she worked herself deeper still into his system.

"I don't need this," he muttered.

Slater threw off the rest of his clothes and headed for

the bathroom. This was one morning he wouldn't complain about how long it took the water to turn from cold to hot in his shower.

SLATER WAS KNOCKING on *her* door this time and telling himself to stay cool. He was after rapport and nothing more. Rapport and nothing more. He repeated the little rhyme in his head, making it his mantra.

"Who is it?"

Her voice sounded small, even weak on the other side of the door. Had being with him brought her down that much? He could already guess what she'd say. She'd talk about how she'd come to his room, let him get next to her, then regretted it. He'd heard that tune before. He'd been singing it to himself ever since he woke up.

"It's Slater."

He figured she'd be more likely to bar the door than let him in. He was surprised to hear the lock click and see the door fling open.

"Come in," she said.

Phoenix grabbed his arm and pulled him through the doorway. He hardly had time to think what was going on. He did have time to notice how lovely she looked in the morning. Last night's moonbeams had been flattering, but he could tell now that she didn't need them to make his breath move deeper in his throat and his muscles tighten below his belt. Rapport, nothing more, he had to remind himself yet again. All the same, he was ready to wrap his arms around her the minute she gave the slightest sign of wanting them there.

"Somebody's been in here," she said.

She shut the door as fast as she'd opened it. After turning the lock and flipping the night latch into place she stood against the door with her back pressed to the dark red-painted finish as if she might be holding the fort against an expected assault. Slater didn't have to look very deep into her eyes to recognize the fear there. He'd seen those eyes frightened before, last night first in the restaurant then again outside his door. This was a different kind of fear. He recognized the edge of panic in it.

"What makes you think that?" he asked.

"I can tell."

Slater looked around. Everything appeared in order, a lot more so than his room would ever be.

"Is this the way you found the place?" he asked.

"Just like this."

"When you got back here last night you decided someone had been in here while you were gone?"

"Not then." She turned away but not before he saw her cheeks redden beneath the pale gold of her beginning tan. He guessed she might be thinking about where she'd been before returning to her room. "Everything was in place last night. I had a hard time sleeping and went for a walk just after dawn. Whoever it was must have come in here then."

Slater nodded. He tried not to think about the thrill it made him feel to hear that she'd had as much trouble sleeping as he did.

"You should be careful about walking around here by yourself when the streets are deserted," he said.

"I thought I'd be safe. Now I'm not so sure."

She bit her lip and looked around the room as he had done.

"What exactly makes you think somebody was in here while you were out?" he asked.

"Things have been moved, things only I might notice." She pulled away from the door suddenly and hurried to the dresser. "I left these earrings on top of my jewelry box, not next to it, and the brush and comb aren't where I remember setting them down, either."

"Maybe the maid moved them."

"Maid service is in the afternoon in this hotel, not early in the morning."

"Maybe you moved those things yourself and don't remember doing it."

Phoenix shook her head. "There are other signs, too. Somebody went through my dresser drawers." She looked at him in a way that insisted he take her seriously. "Especially the one with my underwear in it."

Something about the tone in which she said that made him a believer, and also told him the reason for the sharpness so close to terror in her words.

"Anything else?" he asked, his ingrained cop instincts suddenly alert.

"The closet," she said. "Somebody's been pushing the hangers around and pulling at the clothes, maybe touching them."

She was thinking pervert. He could hear it in her voice. He was thinking of that possibility also, but something else as well.

"What about this Porfiro guy who was hounding you last night?" Slater asked.

"The thought crossed my mind. He certainly has been paying a lot of attention to me, and he does give me the creeps."

"How long exactly did you say he'd been coming around?"

"Only the past couple of days." Phoenix slumped down onto the bed. "But the more I brush him off, the more persistent he gets."

A couple of days was just how long Slater had been

in town here. When he put that two and two together with Porfiro's coincidental interest in Phoenix and her claims of an intruder, Slater couldn't help suspecting that Laurent might be involved somehow. He'd be just the type to put a tail on Slater. If that was the case, Laurent could know where Slater was and what he'd found out. Maybe a backup local had been hired, somebody like Porfiro. Or, maybe Slater was letting his imagination run out of control, just the way some other parts of him had done last night.

"The bartender said this Porfiro is a tour car driver," Slater said. "He hires himself out to guests at one of the big hotels on the road to the airport. Escarpadura is one of the regular spots on his tour. According to the bartender, the *gringos* love the view."

"Did he mention the name of the hotel Porfiro works from?"

Slater thought for a moment. He usually remembered such details, but his head didn't seem to be working at its usual efficiency this morning. He wondered if she might have something to do with that. "He told me which one it was." Slater racked his brain. "I think it had something to do with royalty."

"The Princess?"

"That's it!" He didn't like to admit it, but she seemed to be a better detective than he was at the moment. "Okay. You wait here. I'm going after him."

Phoenix stared at him.

"If you think this Porfiro may have been poking around your room while you were out, I believe you could be right, and that's not something to take lightly. It's at least worth having a talk with the guy."

"I'm not sure it's him."

"He's the only possibility you've got right now. Like I said, I think it's worth a talk with him."

She continued to stare. He could almost hear the wheels whirling between her pretty, slightly sunburned ears. He wished he knew exactly what was going on in there.

"Why would you want to get involved in this?" she finally asked.

"Because I don't think you should be taking this guy on yourself when we don't know how dangerous he might be. Besides, I had pretty good luck with him last night. The only other choice I can come up with is going to the police."

"No police," she said quickly.

Slater almost sighed out loud. Her rapid response confirmed what part of him still didn't want to believe. She obviously had reasons for wanting the law kept out of this. Again, his cop instincts insisted on being paid attention to. She was acting as if she were guilty of something. Most of the time, when somebody did that, they turned out to be as guilty as they looked. On the other hand, everybody was leery of the Mexican police. Slater would have liked to latch on to that explanation, but he knew he mustn't let himself. He had to resign himself to the truth about her whether he wanted to or not.

"Well, if you don't want the cops in on this, then I guess you're stuck with me," he said. "I'm going to check the hotel desk. If it's true that Porfiro brings his tours through here on a regular basis, then they may be able to say for sure if the Princess is the hotel he works out of."

Slater turned to leave. He didn't want to stay here any longer than he had to with the confused thoughts she brought to his mind. He had his hand on the doorknob and was about to tell her not to leave the room or let anybody in until he got back when she came up behind him and grabbed his arm.

"I'm going with you," she said.

"I really think it would be better if I did this alone."

"I don't let anybody do my talking for me," she said with determination in her voice.

He gazed down at her and couldn't help thinking that if he let her get any closer to him he might not be able to refuse her anything.

"But I'd prefer it if you would come with me," she added more gently.

Slater did sigh this time. He nodded, knowing part of him was already putty in her hands. He'd figure out how to get Porfiro on his own after they found him. Then the real questions would begin.

THE YOUNG WOMAN at the hotel desk did turn out to be of help, especially after Slater slipped a fifty-*peso* note into her palm. According to her, Porfiro picked up most of his morning tour business from the Princess Hotel out on the strip at the opposite end of the bay from La Escarpadura, just as Slater had heard. On the way back from La Quebrada, where the famous Acapulco divers leapt from the high cliffs several times a day, Porfiro brought his customers here. Neither Slater nor Phoenix wanted to wait until that happened. They jumped into the Jeep he'd rented at the airport when he first arrived in town.

The morning sun was heading toward white bright already and felt good on his face. He hated to admit that what felt even better was to be sitting next to Phoenix while the wind whipped her hair and the sun shimmered in the golden blond amidst the honey color there. She had on sunglasses, but he could see the look in her wide, blue eyes all the same. She gazed up at him in his mind's image the same way she had last night as she stood outside the door to his room. No matter how many times Slater told himself to stick to business, he couldn't seem to get that image out of his head.

Fortunately, the tiered facade of the Princess Hotel, a modern version of an ancient temple, this time dedicated to the worship of leisure, reminded Slater that today was a workday after all. He wangled a parking spot in the hotel lot by telling the attendant they'd come to look at the place because they were thinking of changing hotels. The attendant looked skeptical until Phoenix beamed a smile on him and said *"Por favor,"* in a silky tone no man could resist. Slater appreciated the assistance, but it pained him to see how good she was at charming men into doing whatever she wanted. Successful criminals often had that kind of charm.

Once they reached the front of the hotel, Porfiro was easy to spot. He was leaning against a dark blue town car with a slick polish that gleamed in the sun. Porfiro looked pretty slick himself. His silver-gray hair waved back from his deeply tanned brow, and he was smiling as he talked to two other tour drivers with cars parked nearby. They must have been waiting to pick up the first tourist load of the day, but it was still a little early for that.

"How about giving me a shot at this guy on my own?" Slater suggested. He anticipated Phoenix's objection even before the frown shadowed her eyes.

"I told you that I don't let anybody do my talking for me."

"That's not what I'm asking you to do. I'm just saying that it's not smart for a woman to challenge a man like this one in front of other men. That kind of approach could force him to make a fight of it. A fight isn't what we're after here, at least not yet."

"What is it we *are* after?"

"We want him to leave you alone."

She studied Slater for a moment then sighed. "All right. Let's see what you can do."

Slater nodded and turned to walk away before she could change her mind. He crossed the wide driveway and strode purposefully toward the trio of men, fixing each of Porfiro's companions with a pointed stare until they couldn't help but notice. Then Slater shifted his gaze back to Porfiro with a scowl. The other two appeared to get the message and faded backward toward their own cars. Under different circumstances, they might have stayed to support their *compadre,* but they worked out of this hotel. Slater had figured they wouldn't want to involve themselves in any trouble that might jeopardize that employment. By the time Slater came face-to-face with Porfiro, he was standing on his own.

"*Buenos días, señor,*" he said with a smile that showed lots of white teeth. "*¿Cómo está?*"

Slater ignored the standard local greeting. "What's your game, *hombre?*" he asked right off, peering straight into Porfiro's suddenly startled eyes. "I thought you got my message last night. Now I have to be back here in your face. I don't like that."

"*¿Qué pasa, amigo?* What's going on?"

"I'm not your *amigo,*" Slater growled, "and what's going on is that you've been dogging the woman I'm with for going on a week now. I want to know who's paying you to do that."

Porfiro looked toward the other side of the driveway

where Phoenix was standing. She took a step off the curb when she saw him, but Slater lifted his hand for her to stay there. Much to his surprise, she nodded and remained where she was, at least for the moment.

"Dogging? *Yo no comprendo*," Porfiro replied.

Slater took another step forward and towered there. "I think you *comprendo* just fine, and I want to know who hired you to watch that woman over there."

Porfiro stole another obviously nervous glance at Phoenix. "You must be mistaken, *señor*," he said as he turned back to Slater.

"I'm not mistaken. When I first saw you at the Escarpadura last night, you were watching her like a hawk, or maybe a vulture. When she told you to leave her alone, you wouldn't do it. I finally had to get your sorry behind away from her myself."

"Oh, well, *señor*," Porfiro lifted his arms in a placating gesture. "Your friend is very beautiful. *Muy hermosa*."

Slater grabbed Porfiro's wrists in a tight grip. "Don't dance me around here," Slater snarled, "or I'll fix it so your next gig will be conducting tours of the Acapulco jail. *Comprende* that?"

Porfiro looked up into Slater's eyes for a moment then nodded slowly. "*Sí, señor*. I understand, but you're wrong about one thing. I'm not working for anybody."

"Then why have you been tailing her so close?"

Porfiro shrugged. "*Mira, señor*. Why do you think I follow her? She is beautiful. She is alone. To me, she looks like she needs company. I did not know she was your territory. I back off now."

"You're not working for anybody? Nobody paid you to keep tabs on her?"

"Nobody, *señor*. Now, why don't you turn me loose."

Slater ignored the request and kept his grip on Porfiro's wrists. "Where were you early this morning?"

"Why do you want to know?" Porfiro was beginning to get his macho up. Slater could see that.

"Somebody searched my friend's room, moved her things around. What do you know about that?"

Porfiro opened his palms from the fists he'd made after Slater grabbed him. "*Nada, señor.* I know nothing about that at all, *señor*. I swear to you. Following a pretty woman around, maybe even bothering her a little is one thing. Breaking into her room is another. I don't want that kind of trouble."

Slater had the feeling Porfiro was telling the truth about that. He might be a lecher, but he didn't give the impression of being a fool. A breaking-and-entering charge would blow this cushy hotel gig for him for sure. He came across as too smart to let that happen.

"You can account for your whereabouts last night?" Slater asked, reverting to lawman lingo.

"I was with the dice and the cards till the sun come. You can ask my two *amigos* about that if you don't believe me."

Slater hesitated another moment before letting go of Porfiro. "I'm going to take your word this time." Slater leaned forward as if to pin Porfiro to the car. "But if you bother her again, I'll make you very sorry."

"You don't have to worry about that, *señor*. I'm not going to bother nobody."

"Make sure you don't," Slater said and backed off then.

"And if I can be of service to you in any way while

you are in Acapulco, *señor,* you know where to find me.''

Slater had begun to walk away but turned back to look at Porfiro who was standing next to the town car now rubbing his wrists and smiling broadly once more. Slater almost smiled himself at the nerve of the guy. Slater nodded.

''I know where to find you,'' he said with a threat in his voice. ''You remember that, too.''

Slater sighed as he walked back across the driveway toward Phoenix, who was still standing there waiting, more patiently than he would have expected her to do.

So, if Porfiro the tour driver didn't sneak into her room this morning, who did?

Chapter Five

SideMan Sax waited until the Jeep left the entrance to the Princess Hotel grounds before pulling in himself. He'd rented a much fancier four-wheel drive than the one McCain settled for. It was bad enough that SideMan had to settle when he was used to a sleek sports car. Unfortunately, the bottom line was that if this mission took him out of town, he might need a workhorse on wheels to get him over the rough spots.

He struck just that pose in his halfway wraparound, opaque black shades and tight fitted slacks. Nobody'd be likely to mistake him for one of these tourist bozos, not if they knew what was good for them anyway. He kept his jacket on when he got out of the car because his pants were too tight for carrying his piece in a pocket. He had it slipped down the back of his waistband. That might have put some guys at a disadvantage, but not SideMan. He'd practiced his draw from the back with a mirror so many times he was lightning fast by now. Lightning fast and lethal. The gunslinger hadn't been born who could get the drop on SideMan Sax.

"Loco gringo," the one with the silver hair was saying to two other Mexicans as SideMan approached. "Trying to shake me down. I tell him nothing, but I

don't give him trouble. No percentage for me in doing that." Silver Hair spread his arms to indicate the hotel and its grounds. "I'm not going to let some crazy gringo take away *mi empleo*."

His two buddies nodded. All three were leaning against a dark blue car with their backs to the driveway and didn't see SideMan until he stepped around the hood of the car.

"What would it be worth for you to take me on a tour right now?" he said to the guy Slater had come close to mixing it up with a while ago.

The guy's silver head shook slowly from side to side. "Sorry, *señor*. I got to wait for the scheduled group out of the hotel here. Starts in an hour or so. You can sign up for that one."

"I'm not interested in one of those group scenes. Maybe this could persuade you to find me a slot in your busy schedule." SideMan slipped the guy a C-note with the numbers folded out so he could see them right off.

The silver head dropped for a minute. When it came up again, the guy was wearing a smile full of store-bought choppers white enough to light a room.

"I am at your service, *señor*," he said.

"Good."

SideMan knew that would be the answer. A hundred bucks American went a long way down here.

"What will be your pleasure this morning?" Silver Hair asked as he held open the back door to the town car.

"Let's just ride around and have a chat first," SideMan said. "What's your name, anyway?"

"Porfiro Sanchez" was the answer. "Your man in Acapulco."

"Good," SideMan said. "I like the sound of that."

In the next hour, Porfiro would prove himself true to his word and then some. As soon as he found out SideMan was after whatever info he could get on the big *gringo* who called himself McCain and his trouble-making woman, Porfiro couldn't wait to help out any way he could. McCain had made himself an enemy, and SideMan was quick to take advantage of that. He even found out about the guy the Farraday broad, who was now calling herself Phoenix, had been trying to look up because he was some friend of her grandfather's from the bad old days. This guy's name was Citrone Blue, and he lived on a side street on the nowhere end of town.

That first C-note was all it took to get SideMan a first-class ride to that street he might have had some trouble finding on his own. Another fifty, and good old Porfiro guaranteed he would be there waiting when SideMan came back out. One look was all he needed to figure out that Mr. Citrone Blue wasn't taking too many first-class rides himself these days. Even more important to know, the lowdown from Silver Hair was that Blue could most likely be bought whether he was down on his luck or not. It turned out this Blue was a well-known character in these parts. As Porfiro told it, Blue was always on the lookout for a buck wherever he could find it.

SideMan treated himself to a sneering chuckle. Laurent had sent him down here with plenty of buying power, and SideMan had used that bankroll well. He'd even bought himself a key to the Farraday chick's room. He'd get one to McCain's, too, when it was needed. Now, in addition to that other good stuff, SideMan had purchased enough information to give him an edge over McCain, including the fact that he thought Porfiro might have been hired to shadow Farraday. That meant Mc-Cain had clued himself in to how he wasn't necessarily being told everything there was to know where Beldon Laurent was concerned. McCain couldn't even be sure he'd been followed. Pretty stupid of him to think for a New York minute that Laurent wouldn't protect his bets and his bucks, but McCain was turning out maybe not to be as smart in the head as he was in the mouth. SideMan chuckled again as Porfiro pulled the town car into the alleyway next to Citrone Blue's building. SideMan liked it when the other guy didn't know where he really stood in a deal. All kinds of mileage could come out of that. He squinted through the dark glass of the car window at the scruffy place where Citrone Blue lived. SideMan liked it even more when the other guy came with a price tag.

PHOENIX FELT A LOT like one of the seagulls over Acapulco Bay, being blown this way then that by each new gust of wind. The lesson of the seagulls, as far as she could figure it out, was to relax and enjoy the ride. Phoenix wished she could take advantage of that lesson. She was in this exotic paradise with a handsome man at her side. If she had any sense, enjoying the ride was exactly what she'd be doing. Maybe she simply wasn't very sensible.

Phoenix had spent the last five years teaching other people how to get closer to wherever it was they needed to be. She could equip them with skills and techniques for giving the impression they wanted to give, but she couldn't transform them into the genuine article. In the meantime, she'd come to wonder what was truly genuine in herself. She'd ended up tutoring a sleazy character on how to make the world think he was squeaky clean. She hadn't realized that was the case when she first took the job, but she couldn't keep herself from recognizing the truth eventually. She left that job finally without so much as giving notice.

She'd drifted into the role she'd been playing in New York, from public relations specialist to consultant to manager of her own business in a field and company she had basically made up as she went along. She'd had no plan. She'd only done whatever came next with no real vision of where she might end up. She'd come to Mexico to put a stop to all of that by coming to a halt in general. Now, she felt herself drifting again, or being carried along by forces beyond her control, which amounted to the same thing. She didn't want that.

"Do you think Porfiro will leave me alone from now on?" she asked Slater, hoping to pin down at least this latest out-of-control situation.

They were driving the Carretera Escenica back toward the city center. The deep blue Bahia de Acapulco sparkled in the sun to their left. Sumptuous homes crowded the descent from the highway to the water. The wild green of Punta Diamante tapered to jutting rocks and a border of sand beach in the distance. Phoenix didn't want to believe that one overzealous creep could ruin whatever chance she might have of actually enjoying this lovely place.

"I've called him off for now," Slater said, loudly enough to keep his words from being carried away by the wind along with the soaring gulls. "Still, you never know for sure with a guy like this."

"But he did admit to breaking into my room this morning."

Slater didn't answer. Maybe he hadn't heard her in the wind. Phoenix held her flying hair back from her face and shouted this time.

"That was a question. Did Porfiro say he came into my room and went through my things?"

Slater hesitated another moment while he negotiated a tight turn on the winding descent toward Acapulco proper.

"Yeah, sure," he answered at last. "That's what he said."

Slater didn't volunteer more. They picked up speed. Phoenix guessed he must be trying to get past this fairly treacherous stretch of highway as fast as could manage that. The wind made it hard to talk anyway. She contented herself with admiring the scenery and then the lively street scene once they were into the town. Back at La Escarpadura, Slater helped her down from the cumbersome height of the Jeep.

"I'm really grateful for your help with Porfiro," she said. "This little mission was definitely beyond the call of duty."

"At your service, ma'am," he said with a mock bow.

Despite the lightness of his tone, Phoenix sensed a distance in his manner. She hoped she was imagining that.

"Please, let me repay you by buying you lunch," she said.

"Thanks, but I think I'm going to catch some shut-eye. I didn't get much sleep last night."

Phoenix felt herself coloring at the implication. Slater shifted from one foot to the other, as if he might be uneasy himself. She guessed he hadn't meant to imply anything about the two of them on his terrace last night. That was simply what came out.

"It's not lunchtime yet," she said, hoping to get them past this awkward moment. "You could nap a while first."

"I really can't have lunch with you," he said.

His tone was too tight to be misinterpreted. Phoenix felt herself coloring higher still.

"Yes, of course. It's your vacation, and you have plans," she said. "I'll let you get to them."

She knew she should thank him again or tell him she'd see him around. Some such pleasantry was certainly in order, but she couldn't get the words to come out of her mouth at the moment. She turned her flaming face abruptly out of his sight and all but ran across the polished terra-cotta patio toward her room. She did her best to fake a casual sort of jogging pace but knew she was failing miserably at that. She was taking flight. Only a fool wouldn't be able to see that.

She was a fool, of course, and she'd just been given the brush-off of the decade to prove it. She and Slater had had a drink and a couple of laughs last night. She'd become the aggressor after that, practically accosting him in his room. Being a man, he'd responded to her advances. Why not? She wasn't that hard to take, at least not for one night and a little hanky-panky. Unfortunately, she'd let herself think of last night as more than that. She was a fool all right.

Phoenix felt tears rising hot behind her eyes. She was almost to the safety of her room where she suspected she might indulge herself in a long cry. She was fumbling with her keys and already beginning to sniffle when a question occurred to her. If he didn't want to see her any more after last night, why had he come to her room this morning? Could the complication of Porfiro have turned Slater off? He didn't seem the type to let something like that influence him one way or the other.

She scoffed aloud at herself for thinking that. "How do you know what type he is?"

She punched her room key into the lock. He was a man after all, and she'd never had much luck understanding male behavior in general. This one was not only a man but a gorgeous man as well. Phoenix spent the next few hours attempting to evict that gorgeous man from her consciousness. Afternoon had come, and she'd managed a furtive nap between blasts of her erratic air conditioner. She was feeling both uncomfortable and disgruntled as she scrambled up on her bed to reach the cord dangling from the ceiling fan. She pulled the cord then stood there atop the mattress for a moment to bask in the breeze from the circling fan blades. She was climbing back down from the bed when she noticed a note under her door. Someone must have put it there while she was trying to rest.

She guessed at once who it had to be from. No one else would write to her besides Slater. She didn't know anybody else in Mexico. She forced herself to walk nonchalantly to the door. The note was on a single sheet of white paper folded over once. She opened it and read through the contents three times before the words came clear to her. Citrone Blue was back in town and had heard she was looking for him. He would meet her at five in the lanai lounge of the hotel.

Phoenix knew she should be overjoyed by this news. She'd come to Mexico to find out more about her grandfather. Talking with Citrone Blue was crucial to that quest. Now she'd found him and all she could think about was that she wished he hadn't set up their meeting at La Escarpadura. She'd rather be far away from here. She'd rather be any place there was no chance she'd run into Slater McCain, not for as long as she lived.

Suddenly, it occurred to her that there was actually a

high probability she'd get her wish after all and never see Slater again. She sighed and sat down on the bed. She couldn't help wishing the note had been what she first imagined it to be.

Chapter Six

Slater told himself he was watching Phoenix because of the assignment. That was partly true, but only partly. He'd been hanging out around the hotel foyer ever since she ran away from him this morning. He'd wanted to go after her and kiss away the hurt he'd seen on her face when he said the cold words he had to say. He'd rooted his feet to the red tile floor instead. He'd finally forced himself to put some distance between them by turning her down flat when she asked him to have lunch with her. He couldn't let himself undo that distance no matter how much he wished he was with her instead of out here on his own lurking behind the one newspaper in English he could find in the hotel gift shop.

He wouldn't blame Laurent for sending somebody down here to check up on what was happening. Slater was turning out to be a poor choice for tough guy. He should have been on the phone to Laurent as early as last night with at least something to report. As for Slater's real assignment, ordinarily, he'd have been further along on that, too. He'd be hot on the trail of the money Phoenix took so maybe they could use that as leverage to get her to give up whatever dirt she might have on Laurent. Slater was dragging his feet on this gig all the way around. He'd made the worst mistake a cop can be guilty of. He'd let himself care.

Now, he had to figure out a way to keep this stall going until he got his head straight about what he should do with this woman he didn't want to turn over, either to the bad guys or the good ones. He could probably keep the Feds at bay by claiming he was pumping her for info on the money and whatever else she might know. In the meantime, he should at least be checking out where the money was *not*. He should have been the one tossing her room this morning, not that the place looked tossed when he saw it. Maybe she'd imagined the whole thing, but why would she do that? She struck him as the levelheaded type. Besides, the slipperiness of the operation put Slater definitely in mind of SideMan Sax. He was the most likely choice for Laurent to send down here to do his hound dogging for him. Slater didn't like the thought of a twisted character like Sax being after Phoenix.

Sax was a piece of work with a twist all right. That's how Slater read him anyway. On the other hand, Sax looked like pretty high-priced talent, maybe too high-priced for playing watchman—unless he had other duties than just watching. What if Laurent had a suspicion Slater wouldn't be up to knocking Phoenix off when the time came? What if Laurent figured he should send some backup for the wet work? Slater shuddered in the gut to think it, especially since his gut also told him what he was thinking could very possibly be true. That's why he was out here in this not so comfortable lobby chair with last week's news held up high enough to hide his face but low enough for him to see over the top of the pages. He was making sure Phoenix didn't get out of here on her own and that nobody got to her, either.

The foyer was really a veranda supported by square, pale pink-colored stucco pillars from the red tile floor to the sloping roof. Breeze drifted through, and birds piped in every pitch from high screeches to low cooing sounds. The flower smell was sweet and heavy especially as midday came and passed. Slater took a few walks around the grounds, always with the entryway to Phoenix's building in sight, to keep from attracting too much attention. Nobody was likely to bother him one way or the other. This was a live and let live kind of place. If a guy wanted to fly all the way down to Mexico and spend his vacation on the hotel veranda while everybody else hit the beach or took in the sights, so be it. Slater liked that attitude, except for the part of it that made this country a tailor-made hideout for criminals. The cop side of him didn't care for that at all.

The cop side of him also didn't care for the way the lazy heat of the afternoon made him want to doze off on the job. Luckily, Slater had clocked enough stakeout time back in his detective days to know all the stay-awake tricks. Still, he'd just about exhausted the lot by the time he spotted Phoenix coming down the path from the corridor to her wing of the hotel. He ducked out of sight through an archway off the veranda which led to a row of coconut palms interspersed with banks of bright flowers.

Those flowers had nothing on her. He could see that plain as day as he peered from the corner of the archway. He could also feel what the look of her did to the inside of him, how she made his pulse race as if he were doing that uphill run he'd thought about this morning. She had on a pale blue dress, soft and cool against the flashy Mexico colors all around her. Her skin glowed golden warm along her shoulders, which were bare except for the thin straps holding up the top of her dress. That top fitted her close but not tight. Tight would have been too obviously sexy. Her style was more subtle than that. She didn't need to come on strong to have every man in gaping distance wishing she was his.

Slater felt himself caught between hating those other guys for having the nerve to gape at her in the first place, and wishing he was the one who had her for himself when it occurred to him to notice she was looking pretty fancied up tonight. The blue dress was simple but not exactly what he'd call casual, and the shoes she had on were the strappy kind that women wear when they're going out somewhere special for the evening. She also had on a long, narrow shawl thing, draped loose across her back and hooked over her elbows so it hung down on both sides. The shawl was lacy and the same creamy color as her shoes. She had on dangly, silver earrings, too. She'd made herself even more beautiful than usual, the way she might look for going out on a date.

That fact clamped on to Slater's stomach and gave it a twist that reminded him he hadn't taken time off from his bird-dogging to have lunch. He'd kept watch over her all day nonstop. Now he had the feeling all that watching had set him up to see exactly what he wanted least to see in the whole world right now, Phoenix with another man. She was headed straight down the path that led to the thatch-roofed, open-air lounge above the bay where there'd be a crowd later on waiting for the sun to set. She wasn't moving at a strolling pace the way this place had a tendency to make you want to do. She was hurrying along, as if she had a purpose in mind, as if she had somebody to meet. Slater sighed hard. At the moment, he didn't have much love for his job. This undercover scene was starting to get him down big time.

"It's a living," he told himself, trying to be smart and offhand. Too bad that particular act wasn't playing anywhere near believable right now. Too bad he had no real choice other than to slip out from his hiding place under the palms and follow Phoenix Farraday wherever she went, even if she happened to be headed for another man's arms.

PHOENIX TOLD HERSELF this was a highlight of her trip to Mexico and wished she could believe that. Slater McCain had robbed the glimmer from any moment without him in it. She'd have to get over those feelings. She'd picked herself up and left her business and her way of life behind in New York City. She could certainly do the same with a man she'd barely known for a heartbeat. They'd had a brief holiday fling, a one-night affair, nothing more. The pain of acknowledging that, even only to herself, seared straight to her soul. The view from the lanai out over the sparkling bay, usually so enchanting, had lost its brilliance for her. Slater had robbed her of that, too. She turned away from the view she'd been so eager for just yesterday.

Phoenix recognized at once that the man walking toward her was Citrone Blue. She'd seen a photograph of him from her grandfather's collection. She didn't recall the features exactly. They'd been faded into graying tones of black and white, a snapshot from a 1950's camera, taken in the glare of too much tropical sunlight for the lens. His bearing was what she remembered, the way he held himself tall and proud, like a military officer or a king. Her grandfather had claimed his friend carried the blood of Spanish grandees, but Phoenix had never believed that completely. As Citrone Blue walked toward her now, straight and elegant with his head held high, she wondered if her skepticism might have been unwarranted. He stopped next to her chair and smiled down at her. He even bowed from the waist before he took her hand.

"You are the beloved grandchild of my dear old friend," he said. "I can see him in your eyes."

He lifted her hand and bent to kiss it in the most genteel manner. She wouldn't have been surprised to hear his heels click together, as well. She couldn't help but be charmed by such old-fashioned grace. His gray hair thinned to baldness at the top of his head. She could see that as he bent over her hand. He'd been the younger of the two in her grandfather's stories. They were both little more than boys then, seeking wild adventures in an exotic paradise. Citrone Blue had been the cohort in those escapades, a young man with enough history already to require the camouflage of an obviously assumed name. He was an old man now. Beyond his refined way of speaking and the ascot tucked so perfectly into the starched, white collar of his dress shirt, she could tell that his youthful recklessness had become the stuff of memory and legend long ago.

"Hello, Mr. Blue," she said returning his smile. She was very happy to see him, much more so than she would have thought just moments ago when her regrets about Slater McCain had crowded all other feelings from her heart. "I'm so pleased to meet you at last."

"The pleasure is entirely mine, my dear." His English was flawless.

Phoenix moved to rise and pull the chair across from hers out from beneath the table so he could sit. He touched her arm before she could do so.

"Stay where you are, my dear." He pulled the chair out for himself and sat down, straight-backed, into it.

"Let me look at you. Your grandfather would have been proud to see how lovely you have grown to be. I will simply have to be proud for him. He would have relished this moment. He spoke so fondly of you so many times."

Phoenix couldn't help but laugh. "He must have been talking about somebody else. I hadn't been born yet when my grandfather was here in Mexico."

"Oh, no." His courtly manner turned flustered for a moment. "My memory has betrayed me yet again. I find that happening more often than I care to say these days. I fear that confusion can too often be the companion of advancing years."

"It doesn't matter." Phoenix wished she hadn't said anything to make him feel so obviously embarrassed. "That was more than forty years ago. I wouldn't expect you to remember what the two of you talked about back then." Of course, she had hoped for exactly that. She understood now that maybe those hopes hadn't been very realistic.

"Forty years," he said and gazed out over the bay as if looking backward to another time. He sat like that for a moment before returning his attention to Phoenix. "Forty years ago must seem like ancient history to one as young as you, my dear."

"I'm not all that young." She thought of thirty as past that designation though she realized it wouldn't seem so to him. "Besides, my grandfather brought his memories so clearly to life for me they felt like they might have happened yesterday."

"Did he tell you many stories of our times together? I would be very pleased to hear…"

The waiter had arrived to take their order. Mr. Blue

interrupted what he'd been saying while Phoenix asked for iced tea and he did the same.

"Yes, my grandfather told me many, many stories of his experiences in Acapulco," Phoenix said after the waiter moved on. "He loved it here, but I'm sure you know that."

"Ah, yes. Acapulco is a special place. I have to hear what your grandfather told you. I am curious to know whether we remembered the old days the same, he and I."

"Well, he talked a lot about how much fun the two of you had." Phoenix searched her mind for specific anecdotes. "I got the impression that you partied long into the night quite often."

"This was an exciting city then, even more so than it is today. Or perhaps it is only the habit of older men to remember the exploits of their youth as if nothing had ever been quite so daring before or since."

He smiled in a wistful, beguiling way that touched her heart.

"That's certainly the way my grandfather remembered things. He did describe this place pretty accurately, though."

"By this place do you mean this hotel in particular?" Phoenix nodded. "He remembered La Escarpadura most of all and the many nights he spent here."

"Looking out over exactly this same beauty."

Mr. Blue turned toward the bay again. The sun was still fairly high. What seemed like its rapid descent toward sunset hadn't yet begun.

"From what he told me, the two of you didn't generally get started here until quite a bit later in the evening in those days."

"Young men tend to prefer the nighttime for their

adventures, especially here in Mexico. That is when the magic happens.''

"My grandfather said the same thing. He told me how even Hollywood movie stars came here. John Wayne, Alan Ladd, even Tarzan."

"Oh, yes, Johnny Weissmuller. This was one of his favorite places. He lived in Acapulco part of the year, you know."

"My grandfather told me that." Weissmuller had a cliff house not far from here as she recalled.

The waiter had returned to set two tall, glistening glasses on the bamboo table next to the terrace rail.

"There are not so many famous faces here now," Mr. Blue said, "but I am not disappointed by that. I would prefer to drink with my friend's beautiful grandchild any day."

He lifted his iced tea high, and she did the same. They were about to make the traditional clink of glasses when a startlingly familiar voice shattered Phoenix's pleasant moment.

"May I join the toast?" Slater McCain stood over them wearing what she had to describe as a self-satisfied grin. "What are we drinking to, anyway?" he asked as if his arrival were completely expected, and she shouldn't feel unsettled by it at all. Unfortunately, that was not the case.

Chapter Seven

Slater could see in Phoenix's eyes how much she didn't want to see him. He swallowed that and stood his ground with a wide smile on his face. He made a couple of remarks about the way they were raising their glasses. The ice didn't break, especially not the ice in Phoenix's eyes, so he tried a different approach.

"Ms. Farraday," he said so enthusiastically he even surprised himself. "How great it is to run into you again. I was afraid we might miss each other."

She covered her frown with a thin smile that didn't look even a little bit sincere. "I was afraid of that too, terrified in fact."

The old guy with her couldn't possibly have missed the sarcasm in her tone. He glanced from her face to Slater's before rising straight up out of his chair as if he had a poker for a spine. Slater had seen the type before, all that blue blood aristocrat stuff on the surface and not two nickels to rub together in the pocket. These guys preyed on anybody naive enough to fall for their Euro-trash line. Slater was surprised Phoenix couldn't see through such phoniness. She was smarter than this.

"Citrone Blue at your service, sir," the old dude said, extending his hand, flashy ring and all.

Slater would have bet big money that if the stone in this bauble ever was a real diamond it had, number one, been a gift from some American woman with too many dollars and not enough sense. Number two, the real rock in question had long since taken up residence with either a pawnbroker or a fence. He took the old guy's hand and gripped it firmly.

"Slater McCain's the name. What particular service did you have in mind?"

Slater felt the guy hesitate after he'd begun to loosen his hand from Slater's. A question passed for just an instant through the old man's eyes. Slater had seen that look before when one man met another and they sized each other up as potential enemies. A slight narrowing of Blue's dark eyes said he spotted Slater for an adversary in the making. They released their grasp on each other at the same moment so neither could think of the other as pulling away. The old guy made a welcoming gesture toward the chair next to Phoenix, as if he were the host of the table and Slater an invited guest instead of the intruder he actually was.

"American humor," Blue observed as Slater nodded and took the seat he'd been offered. "I have always found it so refreshing."

"I'm refreshing all right," Slater declared, assuming the role of *gringo* big mouth as if it were a favorite pair of shoes. "By the way, what kind of name is Citrone Blue anyway? That is what you called yourself, isn't it?"

Slater knew the name perfectly well, of course. Phoenix had mentioned the guy and that he'd supposedly hung out around here with her grandfather in the old days. Slater could spot a phony handle a mile away, and this one was as fake as the guy's glass ring. Slater had already called his Washington, D.C. contact and had him feed Citrone Blue's name into the official checkup system. Chances were it would be coming back with a sheet attached that might more accurately be called Citrone Yellow. Phoenix had been watching the exchange between Slater and Blue with first curiosity then concern on her face, but she hadn't said anything until now. "Mr. Blue is a family friend," she stated. "I'd rather you didn't put him through an interrogation."

"Well, you know me," Slater returned, still putting on the over-jovial act. "Just a natural-born busybody."

"Why don't you try being natural-born polite instead?" Phoenix all but snapped.

"No, no, my dear," Blue said in a tone as soothing as it was slick. "This is a question I am often asked, especially by people like Mr. McCain who take such a delightful interest in the details of the lives of those around them."

The way Blue looked at Slater just then made him wonder if he'd been spotted for a cop underneath the ugly American pretense. He didn't want that. He was supposed to be an ordinary citizen, nothing more, and definitely not a lawman undercover as a bad guy undercover as a *turista*. He'd have to ease up a little no matter how much his first instinct was to lean on this guy until the truth squeezed out. That might be the best way to get Phoenix to see him for what he was and keep herself from being burned by whatever scam he had in mind. It wasn't the best way for Slater to keep from blowing his cover and maybe burning this whole operation in the bargain. He reminded himself one more time that he had to get his head straight and make sure it stayed straight even while the smell of Phoenix's perfume threatened to twist him so far offtrack he might never find his way back on.

"Phoenix is right," he said. "Sometimes I forget my manners. I'm sorry about that."

"You need not apologize, Mr. Slater," Blue said. "I freely admit to having taken an assumed name. I did so many years ago, even before I knew this lovely young woman's grandfather. It was a family situation which prompted me to do so. Politics in the country of my father's birth. All long past now and no longer of any importance. In the meantime, I have become Citrone Blue, and Citrone Blue has become me. I see no reason to change that at this late date."

Slater nodded. It was a good story all right, with just enough mystery to turn on the ladies. He'd be willing to wager a genuine diamond ring that Blue had told this same tall tale many times before, and with great success.

"I think it's a wonderful name," Phoenix said as if right on the old guy's cue.

"Thank you, my dear," Blue said. "It has come to suit me, if I may say so."

Slater felt as if he were watching a performance on-stage, or maybe a soap opera. If this Blue character happened to be a few decades younger right now, this line would probably be his way of seducing Phoenix into his bed. Slater didn't believe that was the game being acted out here today. He also doubted Blue was after Phoenix for her money.

Of course, Slater was aware that she actually did have enough loot to afford a room in the grandest hotel here or anywhere. What she ripped off from Beldon Laurent could set her up in high style anywhere she wanted to be. She was simply too smart to tip her hand in such an obvious way. Was it possible Blue could have a line on how much Phoenix was really worth right now? That didn't seem likely, except that, in Slater's experience, guys like Blue had a talent for sniffing out dough however deep it might be buried. That possibility made Slater wonder if Blue could have had anything to do with the once-over of Phoenix's room that morning. Meanwhile, Blue had signaled the waiter with a single raise of the hand. He arrived just in time to interrupt, quite conveniently, the discussion of the old guy's name.

"What is your pleasure, Mr. McCain?" Blue asked as if inviting yet another smart-mouthed reply.

Slater resisted the temptation to declare that his pleasure would be to pitch this aging con artist out onto the patio.

"Tequila straight up," he said to the waiter instead, "and one for my new friend here, too."

Blue raised his hand again, in a motion that meant halt this time. "Thank you, Mr. McCain, but I must refuse your generous hospitality. My tequila days are past, I'm sorry to say. I must confine myself to less adventurous libations."

Blue indicated the glass of iced tea in front of him and smiled. The savvy glint in his eyes suggested he might have guessed that the tequila had been intended to loosen his tongue. Whether he'd figured that out or not, he wasn't about to fall for the ruse. He might be on the aged side, but he definitely hadn't outgrown his brain power. That would be Slater's assessment at least.

"You say you knew Phoenix's grandfather?" He'd decided to try a different tack. "Just when was that?"

"Back in the fifties," Blue answered. "Acapulco was the place to be in those days."

"Was that the early fifties or later on?" Slater asked.

"I blush to admit I cannot name the exact year," Blue

said with believable humility. "I'm afraid that the longer I am alive, the more those details seem to escape me. In fact, I was lamenting that very same thing to Miss Farraday before you arrived."

Phoenix leapt to his rescue. "It was the early fifties. I remember my grandfather telling me so."

Unlike Phoenix, Slater wasn't about to fall for the fading memory excuse. The smart money said this old guy hadn't forgotten much in his time. If he was playing like he had, maybe that meant he either never knew Phoenix's grandfather at all or at least not anywhere near as well as she wanted to believe. Slater's cop sense told him that was exactly what was going on here. This Blue character was using the pretense of being a dear old buddy to her long lost grandpa in order to get next to Phoenix. What Slater's cop sense couldn't tell him, at least not yet, was how to show Blue up for the sham he was without spooking him in the process. He was a pretty sharp old bird despite his claim of having dulled over the years. Slater decided to lay off for a while and see what happened.

"What was my grandfather like back then?" Phoenix asked.

Slater settled against the seat cushion as if he were only casually interested in the conversation. He wasn't about to let anybody know how hard he was hoping for Blue to slip up here.

"Your grandfather was a wonderful man," Blue said with just the right degree of nostalgic edge to his voice. "I have not had the privilege to know many like him in my time."

"Yes, he was a wonderful man," Phoenix said. "I miss him very much."

Blue leaned across the table and put the hand with the

ring on Phoenix's arm. "Missing your grandfather will be something we can share."

Slater saw the shine in Phoenix's eyes and wished he could tear Blue's hand away from her and knock the guy over the balcony for playing on her most vulnerable feelings the way he was so obviously doing. Slater gripped the arms of his chair to stop himself from committing an action he would regret. He wasn't quite as successful at keeping his mouth shut.

"You must have lots of stories about the two of you back then. How about telling us a few? I'm sure Phoenix would love that."

"Ah, yes." Blue patted Phoenix's arm before easing backward into his chair. "There are so many stories of our times together, Harold and myself."

He knew her grandfather's first name. That was a point in favor of credibility, but Slater guessed Blue could have picked that information up any number of ways, and probably even from Phoenix herself.

"He told me about some of the things you two did together," Phoenix said. "I'd really like to hear your version, too."

"There is nothing I would enjoy more," Blue said. "Those were some of the best times of my life. We were so young then and, I might add, full of mischief." His eyes twinkled as if he might be remembering those escapades right now.

"My grandfather hinted that you got yourselves into trouble on occasion, but he never gave me any details."

"Harold was always the soul of discretion, and you may be assured that I shall not betray him."

Blue smiled so smoothly Slater could hardly stand to look at him. He'd bet his badge this guy was dirty.

"You can tell me," Phoenix said. There could be no doubt that she was deeply hooked on Blue's line.

"I will have to think about that," Blue said. "I am a gentleman after all."

You're a slimeball if I ever saw one, Slater would have loved to shout. He took a swig from the glass the waiter had left on the table. The fiery liquid burned down Slater's throat. Unfortunately, not even tequila was powerful enough to scorch away his disgust with Blue and what he was trying to get away with here. Slater clutched the glass to keep from leaping on this old liar and throttling the truth out of him.

"We will talk more another time," Blue was saying. He'd already begun to rise from his chair.

"You have to leave so soon?"

Phoenix's pleading tone made Slater want to take her in his arms. She'd bought this guy's line of baloney all the way, and she was wearing her heart on her sleeve to prove it. Meanwhile, Citrone Blue was about to make his escape, smooth as silk. Slater's guess was that the seat Blue found himself on had started to heat up once Phoenix began asking questions about the past. Now, he was hustling his behind out of here as fast as he could go. Slater couldn't do anything about it, either, without tipping his hand way more than he had better do.

"I am expected elsewhere," Blue said to Phoenix. "I cannot keep a charming hostess waiting. I will call you in a day or two."

As he spoke, Blue walked around Slater's chair without so much as glancing at him. Blue took Phoenix's hand.

"I will look forward to our next meeting, just the two of us."

Blue's implication that Slater should not be included

in that rendezvous could hardly have been more clear. Blue bent to kiss Phoenix's hand.

"Yes," she said. "Just the two of us."

Blue stepped back and nodded before letting go of her hand with what anybody but Slater would have interpreted as great reluctance.

"Till then," Blue said.

He resumed his ramrod straight posture. As he turned to leave, he favored Slater with a much cooler version of the smile he'd beamed on Phoenix.

"It was a pleasure to meet you, Mr. Slater," Blue said.

He didn't go on to suggest that they should also meet again. Before Slater could decide whether or not to bait Blue further by proposing such a get-together, he was making his swift, straightbacked exit through the crowd of new customers. They were arriving for the cocktail hour followed by the daily ritual of waiting for yet another magnificent Acapulco sunset. Citrone Blue was already out of sight when Phoenix bolted up from her chair.

"Why did you have to come along and ruin that for me?" she cried loudly enough to cause some of the new arrivals to turn around and listen. "I've been waiting to meet that man ever since I came to Mexico. This was my chance to find out more about my grandfather, and you spoiled everything."

"Do you really believe Citrone Blue can tell you those things?" Slater asked.

"Yes," Phoenix said too vehemently for a public place. "I do believe that."

The tears trembling on her lashes made Slater wish he also believed what she obviously wanted so much to be true. He couldn't bring himself to disillusion her more right now, even if she would have listened to him. He watched her hurry out of the lanai lounge and noted that she was headed toward her room, but he didn't follow. Slater signaled for the waiter to bring the check. Four new customers were already lurking nearby, eager to claim the table Slater occupied. He couldn't help thinking that their experience here was almost certain to be more enjoyable than his had been.

Chapter Eight

Phoenix came here to make a new life, or at least to begin one, but this wasn't it. She'd always stayed on top of whatever happened to her for as far back as she could remember. Even when she made mistakes, like signing Beldon Laurent as a client, they were her own mistakes and she accepted full responsibility for them. She also took it upon herself to correct those mistakes. When her research into Laurent's background revealed the kind of man he really was, she resigned the job. She'd never done anything like that before. She liked to finish what she started, but that rule of thumb didn't apply when it came to compromising her ethics. Working for Beldon Laurent, or anybody like him, would take her in a direction she didn't intend to go. She'd said no to that as soon as she saw it happening. Now she was saying no again, but it was a lot harder this time.

Maybe she could use the whirlwind of it as an excuse for the way she'd allowed Slater McCain to walk in and take over her thoughts and, even more so, her emotions. Phoenix had been swept into the vortex of that whirlwind as surely as if a tornado had touched its funnel to her life and set everything about her tumbling out of control. He'd happened to her just that fast, too. One minute she was sitting there minding her own business, the next minute he appeared, and nothing had been the same since.

Of course, Porfiro Sanchez had been involved as well, and Slater helped her out of an awkward situation there. To be fair, she had to give him credit for that, if she cared about being fair right now, which she didn't. All she cared about at the moment was to be left alone. A small voice at the back of her brain told her that *not* wanting to be alone had made her vulnerable to Slater in the first place. She squashed that thought before it barely made itself heard. She wasn't in the mood for reasonable reminders. She was, in fact, in the mood to tear something apart.

Phoenix had been pacing again. It was a habit she'd picked up from her grandfather. She could still remember him, charging back and forth from fence to fence across the narrow yard of their New England home. She could tell how caged he felt just by watching him. As a boy he'd dreamed of wild adventures. As a man, he lived within confines as clearly marked at the fence around his backyard. His short time in Mexico had been the only real freedom he'd ever known. That sad reality was the undertone of every story he told Phoenix about those magical days. Even as a little girl, she'd understood that.

She'd see him lurching from one boundary of his lawn to the other, like an animal in a trap, and all she would want to do was help him escape beyond the limits of those neat, white fence pickets back to the land of freedom and adventure. She'd manage to do that, too, by getting him to tell his stories. She might have heard them dozens of times before. She might even notice the way details, and sometimes even entire scenes, changed from one telling to the next. Phoenix didn't care. All that mattered to her was the way her grandfather took off into his story as if he'd stepped on board a jet airliner and been whisked away. Memory and imagination might mix together at will. The test of harsh reality had never been as important as the story itself and the way it carried both teller and listener on its wings to a more exotic and exciting place than their daily world could ever be.

Her grandfather would stop pacing and hold her on his lap then while the story blossomed around them. She remembered those stories fondly and well, but she hadn't forgotten the way he paced the yard or the frustration that brought that pacing on. She felt herself gripped by that same kind of tension now, driving her back and forth across the tile floor of her room until she half expected to look down and see a path worn there. She wished she could tell herself a story, as her grandfather would have done. Unfortunately, words didn't possess the same calming magic for her that they had for him. Action had always been her antidote to frustration. When things got out of hand in her life, she got moving and did something about it, just like she'd done something about Beldon Laurent. She would do something about Slater McCain, too. She simply had to figure out what that something should be.

Too bad the Beldon Laurent solution wouldn't work here. She'd run away from that situation. She wasn't going to do that again. Being here in Mexico was the beginning of her fresh start in life. She wasn't about to leave. She wasn't going to allow a man, no matter how attractive he might be or how powerfully his presence might act upon her senses, to knock her off the top of her life and out of control. Meanwhile, the memory of just how attractive Slater was and how forcefully he could set her emotions spinning threatened to derail the determination Phoenix was building with each path paced across her room. She knew she mustn't let that happen. Phoenix all but ran out onto her terrace. She grabbed hold of the wrought iron railing and leaned there, gripping it amidst the fuchsia flowers as if to restrain herself from taking off at a fast pace once more. What was it she had to accomplish anyway? She didn't have an answer to that.

"I have to stop this," she said out loud with so much vehemence that a passing seagull was frightened into a banking dive away from her.

Phoenix released her grip on the rail and turned smartly on her sandal heel back into her room. She did know what it was she needed to accomplish after all. She needed to understand. This man had come into her life, then backed away, then charged in again, like a bull in a china shop. Why had he done that? She could understand his first interest and even his second thoughts afterward. What she didn't comprehend was his behavior this afternoon, barging in on her conversation with Citrone Blue and acting like a complete idiot. Ordinarily, Slater came across as much too poised to make a fool of himself that way.

The sharp edge of suspicion nagged at her brain. Something was not quite right here, not what it appeared to be. A blank space needed to be filled in; what was off balance had to be identified and maybe set right before she could even begin to put Slater McCain out of her mind and her heart. She hadn't a clue what that out-of-kilter element might be. She didn't know enough about Slater to begin to figure that out. "But I can correct that," she said and set the seagulls swooping again.

Quickly, Phoenix changed from her sundress to cutoff denims and a pale yellow T-shirt. She slipped the back strap off one of her heels and kicked the sandal across the room. It slid under the bed and was quickly followed by its mate. She grabbed her sneakers from the open closet and pulled them on. She'd need sneaker traction for what she had in mind.

SUNSET HAD PASSED and night was falling fast in its wake. Phoenix was grateful for that. Her plan depended on darkness to succeed. She'd called Slater's room, ready to hang up if he answered, but he wasn't there. That was what she'd hoped for. Still, she couldn't help imagining the sound of his voice rumbling low and throaty along the wires between his room and hers. The buzz of the unanswered ring had been a poor substitute for the thrill she knew she would have felt to hear him say hello.

Phoenix was out her door and hurrying down the corridor before she could think any further about Slater's voice and what it could do to her nerve endings. At the end of the corridor, she slowed herself to a less conspicuous pace and walked down the few steps to the courtyard in front of the hotel office. She didn't take the direct route to her destination, along the walk past the lanai lounge and the restaurant. She'd be observed by too many people that way. Instead, she crossed the courtyard toward the flower gardens. Her sneaker soles squeaked against the smooth, red tiles. The pathway through the gardens was made of rougher stones set into concrete. She could walk more swiftly there than on the slippery tile.

Lights from the tall lampposts shimmered against the deepening velvet dark of the Acapulco evening and brightened the pathway enough for her to see where she was going but little more. That meant no one else would be likely to see her clearly, either. Still, she kept her head tucked down and turned away from the buildings. Late supper talk and laughter drifted down to her. For a moment, she longed to be seated at her usual table with a cup of Spanish coffee in her hand. She hurried faster still, trying to outdistance temptation as she went.

She was out of breath by the time she reached the top of the curving path. The warm, Mexican night had moistened her bare arms with a soft sheen. She was now facing the long building where Slater's room was located. After hesitating beneath the overhanging red tile roof, she moved onto the path which fronted that building. A glance up and down the path and back across the gardens told her the coast was clear. Everyone was inside the restaurant and lounge enjoying the evening among friends and friendly strangers. This was the perfect moment for what she had decided to do.

Phoenix slipped around the corner of the building into the dark shadow of the roof's edge. She moved, smooth as a cat, to the rail at the rear of the building and climbed over it. A stone ledge about a foot wide ran along the cliff side of this wing of the hotel, just as it did along hers. She'd viewed that ledge many times while leaning against her terrace rail on those lonely nights that now seemed too far away to be real. So much excitement had intervened between then and now that she had difficulty imagining a lonely moment.

Phoenix could hardly believe she was standing on that very ledge now, sidling her way along the railing that bordered the terrace to each of the rooms in this wing. Slater was four rooms down. She was busy keeping track of where that would be when it occurred to her that one of these terraces might be occupied. She hadn't considered that possibility when she came up with this plan.

She also hadn't considered exactly how scary it would be sidestepping along this narrow place high above the rocks and pounding sea. One wet, slick spot or single shaky foothold and she could be history. Phoenix felt her stomach tighten and begin to turn. She forced her attention back to the terraces and to her sideways course.

Fortunately for her, the occupants of the first three rooms were either tucked behind their terrace doors or out for the evening. She was grateful for that because she wasn't sure she could survive any delays. By the time she made it to the fourth terrace, her knees had begun to tremble. She grabbed the railing hard and flung one leg over it as the trembling traveled to other parts of her body. That was when she made the mistake of looking down. She hadn't meant to. It just happened, and in that unintentional instant her fate was nearly sealed.

Suddenly, Phoenix was unable to move. She was stuck to that spot by what felt like an irresistible force. One foot dangled above the terrace floor. The other was still on the ledge. She could hear the waves smashing against the rocks below. She could see white, churning foam, just visible enough in the silver moonlight to make the breath catch in her throat. She tried to swallow, but she couldn't manage that any more than she could muster the ability to move.

Phoenix had never realized how terrified she was of heights before. She had no choice but to overcome that terror, at least for the moment, now. To do that would require an act of will. She drew her breath in even more tightly, as if to fill herself with the nerve she needed. She spoke to herself inside her mind so intensely her lips moved. "I can do this," she said, thinking the words slowly and deliberately once and then again. At the same time, she concentrated on putting that dangling foot back on the ledge, then pulling her other sneaker sole free from the ledge while she shifted her weight toward Slater's terrace.

For an endless moment, nothing happened. Then, gradually, a single inch at a time, Phoenix willed herself across the railing. Her gaze stayed riveted to the perilous sea below until the very last minute when her foot was finally planted, solid enough to bear her weight, on the terrace floor. She pulled the other leg over then, nearly falling to the tiles from the numbness that still remained of her terrified paralysis. Her ability to exhale had begun to return when she noticed the damage she'd inflicted on the bougainvillea. Broken leaves and blossoms were strewn along the terrace floor. She scooped them up and tossed them over the railing then did her best to rearrange the vines so the crushed and crumpled section wouldn't show. She was only partly successful in that effort at camouflage. She could only hope that Slater wouldn't notice.

Inside the terrace door, his room was pretty much as she remembered it. He was definitely not a neatness freak, but the place was livable. A long-sleeved shirt, a T-shirt and a pair of dark slacks had been tossed over the back of a chair. Tall, black boots, too warm to be worn in Acapulco, were next to the bed with a pair of calf-length black socks draped over the tops. She pulled open the drawers of the dresser and found them empty except for two pairs of boxer shorts and another pair of black socks. Phoenix resisted the temptation to imagine the briefs on Slater's body.

The closet was equally bare and notable more for what wasn't there than for what was—no bathing suit, no beach clothes, not a piece of warm weather wear to be found. Phoenix looked around the rest of the room. There was no camera or film, no guidebooks, either, not even a tube of suntan lotion, none of the usually essential trappings that go with even the most bare bones vacation in the tropics. She was pondering what that might mean when she heard a key turn in the door.

Chapter Nine

Slater had come back to La Escarpadura. He'd meant to clear his head, but he was as confused as ever. That confusion turned from bad to worse when he opened the door to his room.

Phoenix was sitting on the bed as if she couldn't be more at home. She'd stacked pillows behind her against the headboard and was reclining there as she paged through the sports magazine he'd bought at Kennedy Airport before getting on the plane for Mexico. He remembered slipping that magazine into the drawer of the nightstand after he got here. He hadn't looked at it since. Seeing it now made him wonder if she'd checked out the contents of the dresser and closet, too. She wouldn't have found much if she did. Slater traveled light. He also never wrote anything down. He carried what he had to know in his head, and most of the rest of what he needed was on his back. The khakis, loose shirt and loafer-style shoes he had on were an exception to his usual one outfit plus an extra shirt packing limit. The warm Acapulco weather had forced him to expand his wardrobe for this trip.

"What are you doing here?" he asked.

"I thought we should talk."

"The last time I saw you, you gave the impression you'd rather jump off that cliff out there than talk to me."

Slater watched her closely. He wasn't a big believer in sudden changes of heart. While he was watching, he tried not to dwell on how good she looked in those jean shorts she was wearing. She had her legs crossed, so the shorts rode high up the golden skin of her thigh. He could see just a peek of flesh above the deliberately ragged cuff, but he could imagine the rest. His fingers longed to reach beneath that cuff to the place where more than just the color of her skin was pure gold. He wanted nothing more than to leap on her now and finish what they'd started in the moonlight on his terrace. He might have done just that, but Phoenix swung her legs over the side of the bed and stood up before he could act on what he was thinking.

"What exactly were you up to in the lounge this afternoon?" she asked.

"Do you really want to know?"

"Yes, I do."

She had her hands on her hips, and that made her breasts push out against the front of her T-shirt. He could make out the outline of her nipples. He had to force himself to pay attention to the conversation.

"I was trying to get you to listen to that Citrone Blue character with your head instead of your heart," he said.

"You don't know anything about that man."

"I know a phony when I see one."

"Is that right?" She removed her hands from her hips and curled them into fists at her sides. "Then I imagine you must have a hard time looking in the mirror."

Slater didn't really want to know what she meant by that. He had to ask all the same, just in case her remark had something to do with his being undercover. It wasn't likely she could have found out about that, but he had to check it out anyway. He was about to do that when the phone rang. He was happy to put off what he considered hazardous duty for a while.

"Excuse me," he said as he walked past her to pick up the phone from the bedside table where she'd tossed the sports magazine.

"Hi there, hotshot." The voice on the other end of the line was one Slater definitely didn't want to hear.

"I'm busy right now. I'll have to call you back later."

"I don't think so, sport." SideMan sounded as tough guy slippery as Slater remembered him to be.

"Where are you calling from?"

"A lot closer than I'll bet you'd like me to be. In fact, I'm maybe a mile away from you right now."

What Slater'd dreaded had happened. Laurent had his thug on the trail after all. Slater kept himself from heaving a sigh as he turned away from Phoenix and lowered his voice so she wouldn't hear.

"Where can we meet?" he asked.

"Now you're talkin'," SideMan drawled. "You just hike yourself down to a little club called La Esperanza. It's on the main drag. I've got a feeling you can figure out the rest."

"I'll find it," Slater said. "You wait there for me."

"I'll do that," SideMan said with a sly laugh. Then, he hung up.

Slater hung up also and turned slowly back toward Phoenix. She was watching him with questions in her eyes. He was tempted to grab her right now and drag her out of here to somewhere she'd be safe, but what place would that be? Laurent would just find somebody like Slater to track her down again.

"I'm afraid we'll have to postpone our talk till another time," he said. "I have some business to take care of."

"Is that why you came to Acapulco? For business?"

She didn't sound as if she were asking an idle question. Slater was becoming more certain by the minute that she had suspicions about him after all. She was studying his face intently, and that made him even more uneasy. He'd like to believe she'd come here to his room because she couldn't stay away from him, but he knew better. He also knew he had to quiet her suspicions or she might not be here when he got back from his meeting with SideMan. Slater should want her to stay here because of his assignment, but what he really cared about was keeping her out of danger. He would do just about anything to make that happen, but he'd have to do it without letting her catch on. He walked over to her and put his hands on her shoulders.

"Whatever I came here for," he said, "all that matters now is that I've met you."

This was true, of course. Maybe she heard that truth in his voice because he could see the hardness in her eyes soften just a little before he went on.

"I need to talk to you about us," he said. "I need to talk to you about everything."

She didn't answer. She just kept staring into his eyes as if she might be trying to read something written there. Slater pulled her into his arms, partly to escape that probing gaze. He expected her to push him away, but she didn't do that, not even when he stroked her hair.

"By the way," he couldn't help asking, "how did you get in here?"

"I have my ways."

He thought about questioning her further. Instead, he

said into her ear, "Then, now that you're here, please, don't run away."

She leaned closer into his arms. "I won't," she said.

PHOENIX HADN'T RENTED a car when she first came here because she was trying to keep her expenses down. She didn't have a job to go back to after all, if and when she returned to the States. She'd rented a ride for a day at a time whenever there were specific trips she wanted to take out of town. In between, she depended on the Volkswagen cabs that were everywhere on the streets of Acapulco, even out here. That was true in the daytime anyway. A phone call would be required to bring one to La Escarpadura at this hour, and she didn't have time for that. She didn't have time to change her clothes, either. She was a little too casually dressed for a woman wandering around downtown alone in late evening, whether this was an anything goes kind of place or not. Still, she had no choice. Besides, she had other things to worry about now, things far more important than what she had on.

She circled through the garden just as she'd done earlier, but this time she took the path that led to the parking lot. Slater had left her at the corridor to her room a few minutes ago. She'd stayed out of sight until he was on his way to the parking lot. Then she set out after him. She didn't intend to let him get away without her following, no matter what she had to do. She'd seen him tense up when he got that phone call. She'd heard him arrange to meet the caller, and she was almost certain this meeting had something to do with the truth about why Slater was in Mexico. She also had the feeling that this something meant trouble for him. She couldn't let him go to that trouble alone, even if she had no idea what she might do to help. Phoenix understood that these weren't good enough reasons to break the law, but she was about to do that anyway.

She'd noticed that the gardener always left his truck in the far corner of the parking lot at the end of his day's work. She'd passed by it more than once when she returned from the beach in town in the late afternoon, as she'd done every day until meeting Slater. She'd even noticed that the gardener always left the keys in the ignition. She'd chuckled at that. The truck was in such bad shape that apparently not even he thought anybody would steal it. Of course, the gardener hadn't taken into account how desperate Phoenix would be tonight.

She crouched low on her way through the gardens. Slater headed straight for his vehicle without ever looking in her direction. When she slipped out of the shadows near the gardener's truck, Slater was already inside his rental Jeep. She waited until she heard his motor before she pulled open the truck door, which screeched even more loudly than she'd anticipated. She looked back at Slater's truck and saw smoke coming from the exhaust pipe. The sound of his engine must have covered the noise of the rusty door opening. She yanked the door shut again past where it wanted to stick and felt for the keys in the ignition. She breathed a sigh of relief when she found them there. Phoenix pushed in the clutch, turned the key and stepped on the gas. The engine groaned but didn't turn over. In the meantime, Slater was backing his Jeep out of its parking place.

Phoenix pumped the ancient gas pedal twice and hoped that would help. If she didn't get after Slater soon, he'd be too far ahead for her to be able to follow. She whispered a wish into the night and bit her lip before turning the key to try the gas again. The same groan rasped beneath the paintless hood, but she kept on turning and pumping. The next groan led to another and then the engine caught. She had to crank the wheel around to get out of the parking space. Apparently, the gardener didn't think he needed power steering. She approached the lower exit from the lot just as Slater drove by from the exit at the other end farther up the hill. The old truck bounced out onto the road as Phoenix did her best to accustom herself to the most decrepit vehicle she had ever driven. Luckily, there were enough old cars and trucks on Mexican streets to keep this one from being too conspicuous. No one would pay much attention to Phoenix jolting down the hill in pursuit of Slater's taillights. No one but Phoenix would know that she had just undertaken what was maybe the most foolhardy thing she'd ever done in her life.

THE ESPERANZA CLUB was exactly the kind of sleazy dive Slater would expect SideMan to hang out in. The walls and ceiling were painted black with some red here and there. At least, that's what it looked like through the near dark and the haze of cigarette smoke. The small tables and especially the bar area were fully occupied by the lowlifes Slater's cop side was way too familiar with. He'd bet his last *peso* that if he pulled a raid in here right now he'd come up with a couple of dozen righteous collars out of this one room alone.

Slater threaded his way past women who looked him over and petty hoodlums who did the same. He avoided eye contact with all of them, while the hairs on the back of his neck prickled from how much he didn't like being in this kind of place where trouble lurked in every corner and behind every tough expression. He was relieved to spot SideMan at a table near the wall. He looked as if he'd found his natural habitat, just as Slater expected he would. SideMan leaned back in his chair in a cocky posture that made him look as if he were swaggering even when he was sitting down. Slater felt his palm itch to slap the smug smirk off this creep's skinny face. Slater had to remind himself to stay cool. He hated dives like this, where SideMan was obviously so much at home. That could give him an edge, so Slater had to be careful.

"The hot ticket has arrived," SideMan drawled in his usual sneering tone.

He didn't get up.

He would be too short to look Slater in the eye if both of them were standing. SideMan trained his disdainful gaze somewhere around Slater's belt buckle for a fleeting moment then looked away with another sneer.

"Sit down," SideMan said. "It must be a drag carrying that load around."

Slater ignored the mocking reference to his height and breadth, except to say, "We all look the same size to a bullet."

"Hey, there. You're feelin' tough tonight," SideMan observed with a snide laugh as Slater pulled out a chair and sat.

"That must be because I brought along my two pals, Smith & Wesson."

"Did you really?"

If the suggestion that Slater was carrying a gun had any effect on SideMan he was sneaky enough not to let it show. Slater didn't respond.

"Funny you should bring up the subject of packin' heat," SideMan said, "because I have a little present here for you from Mr. Laurent."

"Oh, gee. And it isn't even my birthday."

"That's right, big guy. And I ain't the Easter Bunny, either."

"So, what you got for me?"

Slater could hear how easily he slipped into sounding like a lowlife character himself. The job required it, and he had the talent. It was a talent he took no pride in. He continued to wonder how far he really was from being a piece of street garbage himself.

"I got something you're going to need real soon," SideMan was saying.

He had a package in his lap, something wrapped in a cloth. He tossed the wrapping off and picked up the gun that was inside. Slater's hand shot instinctively to the back of his waistband.

"Relax, cowboy," SideMan said with another sneering chuckle. "You really are on a short leash, aren't you?"

He sounded arrogant and unconcerned as usual, but he turned the gun barrel away from Slater all the same before pushing it toward him.

"Don't you think you should at least try to keep that out of sight?" Slater asked.

"In this dump?" SideMan shrugged. "I'd bet there ain't half a dozen guys in here travelin' light."

Slater looked around. If anybody'd seen what SideMan had in his hand, they weren't taking obvious notice. Still, Slater's cop sense told him there were a whole lot of *hombres* watching out of the corners of their eyes. And, just like SideMan said, they most likely weren't light on firepower.

Slater took the gun and slid it under the table. He'd gotten only a glimpse of it in SideMan's hand, and Slater couldn't see it very well in the dark under the table. He didn't need to see it anyway. He could tell by the heft and the feel of its shape that it was a .38, the standard-issue police pistol. His fingers clenched around the taped-up grip. He knew how possible it was that this piece had been stolen off the body of a dead lawman.

"Clean as a whistle," SideMan said. "Serial number's been lasered off so deep not even the Feds could pick it up. It's got no history anybody could trace anywhere we'd care about."

Maybe it could be traced somewhere I'd care about, Slater thought.

"Why are you giving this to me?" he asked.

"A job needs doing here, and Laurent picked you to do it. Not my choice, but I do my job, too. So, like they say, a mechanic's only as good as his tools. This here's a really good tool."

Slater knew what SideMan meant, of course. Slater had been hired to find Phoenix, then to kill her. He never intended to do that, but he'd had no personal feelings about it in the beginning. Now, to hear the suggestion again made him feel like yanking this creep up out of his chair and strangling the sneer off his face right here and now. Keeping cool was getting harder for Slater by the minute. He had to remind himself he was a cop first and foremost, and that undercover meant hiding his feelings as well as his identity.

"Laurent sent you all this way just to bring me this piece?" Slater asked.

"He wants to make extra sure you've got what you need."

"I guess that makes you a really high-priced delivery boy then, doesn't it?"

Slater knew it wasn't particularly wise to rile this guy. Playing him along would be a better way to get the job done, but he couldn't pass up the opportunity to see

SideMan's face twist like it was doing now. The reaction lasted only a minute, then he was sneering again.

"You think you can get a rise out of me, don't you?" SideMan said.

"To tell you the truth, I don't think much about you at all."

SideMan pounced forward out of his wise guy posture to put his face just inches from Slater's.

"Well, you'd better think about me," he snarled. His tone was low and evil, and his eyes were full of hate. "Because I'm going to be doing a lot of thinking about you."

"That makes me feel warm and cared about all over," Slater said in a calm, steady voice. "Now, get back out of my face."

He didn't say what he'd do if SideMan failed to comply, but the threat hung in the air between them anyway. SideMan held his ground a minute more, just long enough to protect his ego. Then he snorted his usual derisive laugh and eased back into his seat.

"I don't need to pick a fight with you now," he said. "I'll just hang around and see what happens. There'll be lots of time for fighting if you don't do what the man says."

"So, you're not just Laurent's delivery boy. You're his watchdog, too."

SideMan looked as if he were ready to pounce again, but he kept his cocky pose.

"Don't push it," he said.

"Why should I?" Slater pushed his chair back and stood up. "I'm like you. I don't need to pick a fight right now. I'd rather do that at my own time on my own turf."

"Name the place," SideMan sneered. "I'll be there."

"You can count on it," Slater said.

He'd slid the .38 into his jacket pocket before standing up. He had his 9 mm pistol in his waistband at the small of his back as usual. He could reach it fast if he had to but probably not if he was walking away. He backed off a few steps. Now he'd have to turn around and walk out of here. That was part of this macho standoff game he and SideMan were playing. Slater would have to assume it wasn't in SideMan's best interests to make Slater a corpse just yet. Still, he had his breath sucked in the entire time he was walking through the swarthy crowd of the patrons of La Esperanza. Slater didn't breathe freely again until he hit the street.

He took a minute then to wonder why SideMan hadn't mentioned the money Phoenix was supposed to have stolen and whether Slater had any clues to where it might be. Maybe SideMan was just too busy being a punk to remember the bottom line. He was a punk for sure. Even the torrid Acapulco night felt fresh and cool after breathing the same air as SideMan Sax.

PHOENIX HAD PARKED down the street. The Mexican kids who usually tried to get *gringos* to pay them for guarding their vehicles took one look at the truck and didn't bother. She'd hesitated at the door of the club called La Esperanza. She could tell it was the kind of place she shouldn't be in at all, and especially not by herself. She went inside anyway. She did her best to ignore the remarks coming from men on all sides as she maneuvered among them. When one of them offered to take her to a table and buy her a drink, she brushed past him. She spotted a stairway leading to a balcony and decided that would give her the best view of the room. Once she was up the stairs, she kept as far back as possible from the rail. She wasn't likely to be seen here from the floor below. Most of the balcony tables were empty so she didn't have to listen to males trying to come on to her, either, and that was certainly a relief.

She eased a little closer to the rail and peeked over. She spotted Slater right off. He was easy to pick out, even in this darkened place, maybe because he was the best-looking and the biggest man in the room, at least that was how Phoenix saw him. He was with a man who was sitting too far into the shadow of the balcony for Phoenix to see him clearly. Then, he darted forward. She was about to check him out more closely when something else caught her attention and held it. She'd thought he might have handed something to Slater a moment before. Now, she saw that something in Slater's hand as he moved it out from under the edge of the table.

Phoenix stepped backward against the balcony wall. She didn't want to believe what she had seen. The darkness could be playing tricks with her eyesight, but something told her that wasn't true. This sleazy place full of dangerous-looking men, Slater in a late-night rendezvous with heaven knows who or what, the fact that Slater obviously hadn't come to Acapulco to soak up the sun— it all added up to confirm that what she'd just seen was the glint from the barrel of a gun in Slater's hand.

Chapter Ten

Slater had taken the gun with a desperate wish that, if he had it and SideMan didn't, Phoenix might be safe from harm. That made no sense, of course, and Slater knew it. SideMan would have an untraceable weapon of his own, or maybe he wouldn't care about whether it could be traced or not because it wouldn't come back to him anyway. He'd obviously come here to watch Slater more than to give him the gun in the first place, to watch him and to make sure he did the job he was hired to do. Except that Slater was actually assigned by his real bosses in Washington to look as if he were following Laurent's orders when he wasn't. With SideMan in Acapulco, that would be a lot harder to manage, especially since Slater was coming to believe that his true boss had to be his own heart. His heart told him he must protect Phoenix from danger and everybody else be damned, if that was the way it went.

How he would go about protecting her was another problem. He could feed her some knockout drops and kidnap her, but he'd have a hard time getting her out of the country that way. Ordinarily, his D.C. contacts could arrange a back door exit from just about anywhere, even with a less than conscious travel mate in tow. Too bad they wouldn't want to do that in this case. Their best interest was served by keeping Slater and Phoenix exactly where they were, and the types he worked for always served their own best interests first.

Maybe he should confront her straight on, tell her what he knew and why he was here and convince her to cooperate. He had a feeling that would be his only choice eventually. Then the hard decision would be whether or not to tell her everything, the official truth beneath the cover story about San Francisco and the undercover deal with Laurent. Slater had never thought seriously about blowing his cop cover to anybody before. As a matter of fact, he'd never even considered it half seriously. He could hardly believe he was doing that now. The difference was Phoenix. With her around, the undercover game and his attitude toward it had suddenly changed. He wasn't even sure he still wanted to play.

Slater had pulled the Jeep into the parking lot of La Escarpadura several minutes ago, but he was still sitting behind the wheel. He gripped the stick shift then let go, like he used to do with a flex ball he'd carry in his pocket and squeeze when he was feeling agitated. He hadn't carried that ball in a couple of years. He'd been a time bomb waiting for a place to detonate back then. He'd thought he was over that. Now, here he was, clutching and releasing again because, if he didn't, he might drive back downtown to find SideMan Sax. There'd be no telling what Slater would do after that, and maybe no controlling it, either.

He'd slid way down in the seat with his head leaned against the high seat back when the sound of an engine without a muffler invaded his unsettled thoughts. Slater glanced in his rearview mirror to see a very old pickup truck chugging and smoking its way toward the far end of the lot. They've got no such thing as emissions standards in Mexico, he thought. Mexico didn't have many standard regulations about anything at all. He'd left American-style law behind on the other side of the border. He was on his own here where any badge he'd ever carried wouldn't count for much.

He shoved the Jeep door open with a sigh and stepped out onto the gravel lot. He flexed his shoulders and stretched his neck to release some of the tension there. He looked up to see the sky was dark and clear, the stars seeming to shine through it like hundreds of silver pinholes in black velvet. How beautiful it was. He was thinking about how much he'd like to bring Phoenix out here to gaze at the stars with him when he heard a scuffling footstep across the gravel parking lot and there she was. Apparently, she'd decided not to wait for him after all. She had her head down now and didn't appear to have noticed him where he was standing between the cars. The way she was dressed, in the same shorts and sneakers she'd had on before, made him think she'd been out for a walk.

"Isn't it a little late for a stroll?" he asked, stepping from between the vehicles.

Her head jerked up. She stared at him, as if she couldn't see who he was.

"It's me, Slater," he said, feeling a little foolish.

Obviously, she'd been thinking about something other than him. This wasn't the first time he'd wished he could crawl inside her thoughts. He almost asked her what they were, then decided against it. If he asked her to come clean, she might want the same from him. He slammed the Jeep door instead and walked toward her. He could tell how uncertain she was by the expression on her face.

"You look like you're about to run away on me," he said.

"I didn't expect to see you here." She sounded as off balance as she looked. "I thought you would have gone in already."

"What made you think that?"

She shifted from one sneaker to the other and bit her lip before answering. "Your meeting in town," she said. "I figured it would be over by now and you'd be back in your room."

"Almost, but not quite," he said. "How about a nightcap in the lounge?"

"Did you want to have that talk you mentioned earlier?"

"What talk was that?"

"You said you wanted to talk about us."

She appeared to be more under control now, while he was suddenly feeling uneasy. He did remember saying that to distract her from asking where he had to go after Sax's call, and to keep her from running away again. He shouldn't have suggested something he was so totally unready for.

"We could do that," he said.

She studied his face for a moment, as if she might be able to see the doubt and questioning there.

"Maybe some other time," she said. "It's been a long day. I need to get some sleep."

She did look tired. That could be part of what had made her appear so puzzled a moment ago.

"A long day," he repeated. "It has been that."

"Good night, then."

She started to walk away, more hurriedly than she'd been moving before.

"Let me walk you to your room."

"Not tonight," she said over her shoulder. "You go have your nightcap."

She kept on walking, still hurriedly, too much so for him to call after her that he'd never really wanted that nightcap at all.

PHOENIX BARELY HAD the energy to get herself out of her clothes before falling into bed. She wanted only to be unconscious, and soon she was. Whatever thoughts may have plagued her through the confusion of the day were lost in oblivion. She would have been happy to leave them behind, though happiness was probably not an emotion she could manage at present, whether she was waking or not. Melancholy was what she'd felt as she fell into exhausted sleep.

That melancholy stayed with her through the night, along with something else, something that even intruded upon her dreams. Morning was near, maybe even already dawned, and still she felt it. Even as she slept like a stone, hardly moving, it was there. She was afraid. Then, she heard something, though she didn't know if the sound came from her dreams or from the waking world. It sounded like a shutter banging, the way the shutter would bang sometimes in her bedroom at her grandfather's house. She reached out for that room, tried to turn the course of her slumbering senses in that direction, while the bang of the shutter grew louder.

She forced herself awake, or partly so. She could see the light through her eyelids even before she opened them. The images of sleep and dreaming were gone, but the emotions she had experienced then were not. She was still gripped by fear. The sounds were still with her also, at least the rapping noise. Gradually, she knew that wasn't a dream. She sat up and dragged one leg at a time over the side of the bed. She still had on her T-shirt and panties. The fear and melancholy of the night lost some of their hold on her as she rose to her bare feet. She felt the tension and sinking sensations fade as she stood there wondering what she'd meant to do next.

The rapping was at her door. She realized that eventually. Had she ordered breakfast in the room? She'd done that a couple of times, hung the long card on her doorknob at night with her selections checked off. Orange juice, coffee and oatmeal with brown sugar were her usual choices. She was hungry all of a sudden. Had she eaten yesterday? She must have, but she couldn't remember when. She could picture the brown sugar melting into sweet pools on top of the hot cereal.

"Just a minute," she called out as she stopped to grab her robe from the foot of the bed and throw it on.

She pulled the door open as she was tying the cord to her robe. She was about to tell the waiter to carry the tray out onto her terrace while she got a tip from her dresser drawer when she saw that it wasn't the waiter at all. Standing on the threshold of her room was Slater McCain.

"You shouldn't open your door like that without finding out who's knocking first," he said as a greeting.

"I thought you were food."

He laughed, a deep and full laugh that reminded her of that melting brown sugar again, except that she was the one melting this time.

"I'm not food," he said, "but that *is* why I'm here. Let's go to breakfast. I'm starving."

The events of last night were drifting back to her now, drowning out the seductive rumble of his voice. Phoenix looked away from him. She couldn't stand to see how wonderful he looked, or how just finding him there at her door had made her smile before she could remember why she shouldn't be smiling.

"Throw some clothes on. We'll drive into town and find a breakfast place on the beach," he said.

She opened her mouth to babble some excuse why she couldn't do that, but he cut her off before she could manage a word.

"No arguments," he said. "We both have to eat. The sun is up. Let's go find fresh-squeezed orange juice and the best coffee in Mexico." He hesitated before adding, "Maybe we can have that talk we didn't have time for last night."

Last night was what Phoenix didn't want to think about. Then again, maybe talking would bring some answers to her questions, like the big question she found herself unable to stop asking, the one about the gun. She shuddered at the thought.

"You're shivering," he said. "You need to get your clothes on and come with me."

He stepped forward, as if he might be thinking about chafing her arms to make her warm. Phoenix backed away from him. She was confused enough already without letting him put his hands on her.

"Please, wait outside," she said. "I'll only be a minute."

She realized she was going along with him to get away from him. That didn't make much sense even for someone so recently snatched from a much needed sleep, but she couldn't think of an alternative. She needed to find out things, and she couldn't do that without talking to him. She also couldn't go much longer without eating or she might faint dead away. Two birds with one stone was what breakfast with Slater would be. She told herself she could make certain it was nothing more than that as he backed out of the room to keep her from hitting him with the door she was closing in his face.

SLATER STARED AT the dark red door and contemplated how much force he would need to apply to shove it off its hinges. He didn't really believe she intended to go to breakfast with him. She'd only said that to get him out of her room. She'd lock herself in there now, slide the night bolt, maybe even prop a chair back under the doorknob. He could still get through, but probably not before she had time to call for help, if she carried trying to get rid of him that far. He'd have to risk it anyway. If she wasn't out of there in five minutes, he'd start knocking again. If that didn't work, he'd start shoving. She couldn't go anywhere, after all—or could she?

He'd already figured out how she got into his room last night. The damaged flower vines on his terrace told that tale. She must have walked along the narrow ledge out there and climbed into his room. That was the only explanation for her getting in without a key. His door had been locked when he got back there last night and found her, just like her door was locked now. If she'd had the nerve to walk along that ledge last night, she'd have the nerve to do it again this morning. He wasn't going to give her five minutes after all. Slater lifted his fist to knock one more time before he had to start shoving. The door opened just at that minute, and Slater found himself punching a knock against thin air.

She'd put on jeans and a clean blue T-shirt and the same sneakers he'd seen her in last night. Her hair was combed, but she couldn't have had time for much else in the way of making herself beautiful. He marveled at how beautiful she was anyway. The sleepy softness was still on her cheeks, and his fingers itched to touch her gently there. Her eyes, not so morning soft any longer, told him he shouldn't do that. She turned away to lock the door behind her, and he couldn't help but notice the way her jeans fit close over the roundness of her as she bent slightly to turn the key. In that instant, he remembered how he woke up that morning wanting her so badly he could barely stand it.

"Do you know any good breakfast spots downtown?" he asked to keep himself from thinking any further about what he was really hungry for.

"Any place that's open along the Costera should do, or we could eat right here."

"Let's try someplace different," he said. "Maybe along the beach side downtown."

She nodded but didn't say anything. They were on their way down the corridor now. She was walking as far away from him as she could without bumping against the opposite wall. He wondered why she'd come along at all. Maybe she'd figured out that he intended to come busting in after her if she didn't. Could she know him that well already, well enough to pick up on what he was thinking even through a closed door? Maybe so. He could tell what she was thinking right now. She was wishing she could be somewhere else, probably anywhere else as long as he wasn't there. Slater didn't need any extrasensory powers to guess that. All he had to do was look at the way she was walking with her back as stiff as a board and her eyes straight ahead to tell that she wasn't exactly enjoying his company.

They were down the steps to the patio now and headed for the parking lot. He was trying to come up with something to say that wouldn't sound too stupid. He'd discarded, "Did you sleep well?" and was searching for another possibility when she picked up speed. He had to hurry his pace to catch up. She was onto the gravel of the parking lot as he did. He reached out to catch her arm, and she dodged away from his touch as if his hand might be a red-hot poker or a stinging cactus.

Slater didn't even have the second it would take to register how crummy her jumping away from him like that made him feel. At almost the same instant she moved, something zinged through the space between them and hit the ground behind, spitting up gravel in a quick burst. Slater's reaction was automatic. He dove for Phoenix and knocked her forward and down underneath him between the two closest vehicles.

"What the—" she began, already struggling to get away.

He thrust his hand over mouth. "Somebody's shooting at us," he whispered in her ear. "We have to keep down and keep quiet."

Her struggling stopped, as if she'd frozen suddenly to stone beneath him. Even her breath stopped against his hand. He moved his hand away from her mouth but remained ready to smack it back again if she started to scream. She whispered instead.

"I didn't hear a gunshot."

"Silencer," he said.

He was surprised she didn't react to how improbable that must seem to her. Unfortunately, Slater didn't find it improbable at all, even on this otherwise lovely Acapulco morning. His guess would be a .22 caliber with a silencer, just like he'd said, with SideMan Sax doing the shooting. Slater could even guess the reason. He was being put on the hot seat, hotter than the gravel beneath them now. SideMan was delivering a message for Beldon Laurent. Get down to business, fast, that message said, and Slater couldn't help hearing it loud and clear. A warning was what this had to be. Otherwise, Sax's aim most likely would have been dead-on.

Chapter Eleven

Somebody was shooting at him!

Phoenix's first instinct was to roll out from under Slater and throw her body over his instead of the other way around. She mustn't let anything happen to him no matter what. She was surprised by how strongly she felt that. She was equally astonished by how unsurprised she felt to learn that somebody was shooting at him in the first place. What she'd seen last night had already led her to conclude he was mixed up in something criminal. Most shocking was the fact that, right at the moment, she didn't care about the criminal part at all.

Slater lifted gradually from on top of her, and that was when her elbows and forearms began to sting where she'd scraped them on the gravel as she fell. Slater inched forward in a crouch between the cars.

"Be careful," she said as insistently as can be done in a whisper.

"He's gone," Slater said after a minute. He had pulled halfway out of his crouch and was scanning the top of the incline near the building where his room was located.

"How do you know it was a he?" Phoenix asked.

"I just know."

"Do you know who the man was?"

"I have my suspicions."

Phoenix had been right. Someone was after Slater, and he knew who it was. That meant it had to be somebody he'd been associated with. She had scary visions of some kind of underworld deal gone wrong. She wished she could whisk Slater straight out of here. She was thinking about where she might whisk him to as she sat up and began picking bits of gravel out of the abrasions on her arms. She couldn't help wincing as she did. Slater continued to scan the top of the rise near the buildings.

"How do you know he was up there?" she asked.

"From the angle of the bullet. Or, maybe it was bullets. I heard only one."

He knew too much about firearms for a regular person. He sounded too calm, also. This kind of incident wasn't new to him. At least, he didn't act as if it were. He turned back toward her, and she saw that he was holding a gun. She gasped.

"Don't worry. I won't use it on you," he said. "It's for the bad guys."

Phoenix didn't want to believe he was one of those. She tried to smile, and that was when she realized how hard her heart was pounding.

"Look at your arms!" he exclaimed as he crouched back down at her side. "That must hurt."

Not as much as if I'd been hit by one of those bullets intended for you, she was thinking. It was dangerous to be with this man. She should get away from him right now, but she knew she wouldn't.

"We need to clean these up," he said as he surveyed her scraped forearms. "They must have a first aid kit in the hotel office."

"Let's not get the office involved," she said. "They'll make a big fuss."

"That's true. They'll be worried about a lawsuit."

He was really very cynical. She wondered if he'd been that way before and she just hadn't noticed. What she did notice now was that he hadn't said a word about reporting this attack to the police.

"I have some Mercurochrome in my travel bag," she said. "I can clean these cuts myself."

"I'll do it," he said. "After all, it's my fault you have them."

She stared at him. Was this his way of trying to tell her the truth about himself?

"Because I had to push you down on the ground like that," he added.

"If you hadn't, I might be dead right now."

The truth of those words was startling, even more so because, despite that truth, she still had no intention of running away.

He helped her up, and they headed back toward the hotel buildings. He leaned protectively over her as he kept watch in all directions around them. He still had the gun in his hand but tucked close to his side and between them so it wouldn't be so noticeable to the few people out here this early. Acapulco tended to be a late-night town so there weren't many potential spectators at this hour. The two people they did pass watched with some curiosity as Phoenix and Slater moved in a crouch across the parking lot and hurried toward her corridor. She avoided the curious glances and was relieved when she and Slater reached her room and could shut the door behind them.

"Where's that Mercurochrome?" Slater asked.

He'd put the gun away, and that was another source of relief for Phoenix.

"On the bathroom shelf," she said. "In my toiletry bag."

He went into the bathroom. She could hear him rummaging around in there as she sat down on the bed and contemplated what to do next.

"I found it," he called. She could hear the water running.

"You should really come in here where I can wash those cuts out better."

Phoenix tried to answer but found herself suddenly lightheaded.

"You're white as a ghost."

He'd come out of the bathroom with a wet washcloth in one hand and her bottle of Mercurochrome in the other. He put both down on the dresser then hurried to her side.

"Lean your head down between your knees," he said.

He pushed her body gently forward, and she complied. She was feeling queasy and was grateful for any help he could give.

"You're having a delayed reaction to what happened out there," he said.

Just as she'd noticed before, he acted as if being shot at was old hat to him. Well, he might feel that way, but she was scared. She was especially scared for him.

"We have to get out of here," she muttered with her head still between her knees.

"What did you say?"

She straightened up a little too rapidly and saw pinpricks of light darting in front of her eyes for a moment.

"We have to get out of here," she said in a voice she wished she could make stronger. She anticipated that he would need some convincing. "We have to go some-where safe."

"Did you have any place specific in mind?" He actually sounded as if he were considering her suggestion.

"I do know a place," she said.

She also knew she would do whatever was necessary to get Slater to go there.

PHOENIX ALREADY had a hideout in mind. The implication wasn't lost on Slater. Only somebody on the run would bother to think out an escape route ahead of time. That would have turned him totally against her two days ago, but he'd changed since then, at least where she was concerned. Still, he couldn't help but notice how she'd reacted to the shooting incident, or more significantly how she'd failed to react. She didn't appear particularly surprised to have somebody after her with a gun. She never mentioned going to the police, either. Instead, she'd swung directly into her escape plan smooth as clockwork.

She insisted they take nothing with them because leaving the hotel with bags would attract too much attention. She suggested stopping for a few things on the road, and Slater went along with her. Meanwhile, he'd have to be careful they weren't followed wherever it was they were going. Phoenix wouldn't tell him their exact destination. She would only say that they were headed out of town and she'd give him directions along the way. She obviously knew what she was doing. After that moment of faintness back in her room, she'd turned cool as a cucumber. She'd even thought out that they should stop at an open-air market on their way out of town to pick up the things she'd mentioned back at the hotel. Slater wasn't surprised when those purchases turned out to be the basics of a disguise—very dark glasses, large hats, oversize shirts that would conceal body shape.

Slater watched the street while she shopped. No sign of SideMan or the kind of ride he'd most likely drive. It was still early in the day. There weren't many non-Mexicans out and about as yet. SideMan's pasty paleness would be very noticeable in this crowd. He wouldn't actually want to kill Phoenix, of course, not before Laurent's money was located. Still, Slater wanted to get her out of circulation. There was no telling what SideMan did have in mind next, except that it probably involved some tightening of the screws very soon. Out of town was the place to be when that happened.

PORFIRO COULD SEE the big guy clear. He was checking out the street as if he had his head on a swivel, but he didn't see Porfiro. That made him smile. If he'd brought the town car, it would be a different story. He'd stick out like a red thumb in that big, fancy car here by the market at the corner of La Costera this early in the morning. His Chevy was so old and ordinary nobody would notice it, but it was good enough to get him wherever the big guy and the *señorita* might be headed today. Then Porfiro would call the number in his pocket and report where they were, just like he was being very well paid to do. This wasn't all about money, though. Porfiro didn't like the way the big guy had treated him that morning outside the Princess. Porfiro deserved respect. When he didn't get it, he did not forget. He was happy to help the *gringo* Sax even though Porfiro could tell Sax was as *loco* as they come. He was down on the big guy, and that was okay with Porfiro. Besides, the pay *was* good.

"ARE YOU SURE you know where we're going?" Slater asked.

"I'm sure."

Phoenix had been out this way before on one of those days when she'd rented a car. Very few Europeans and almost no Americans came out here, especially this early in the day. The familiar streets of Acapulco, with two-story buildings side by side along every block had given way to shabby houses canted off hillsides. The ocean sparkled off to the left, but the rest was fairly barren except for clumps of vegetation and trees.

"We don't have much farther to go," she said, "and it's very different from this where we're headed."

She directed Slater down a road to the left off the main highway, and almost immediately the landscape changed. Small, mostly single-story buildings lined both sides of the road, some with colorfully painted signs and illustrations on their adobe walls. Bowers of vines and bright blossoms formed archways toward the sea which was briefly visible at a distance between the buildings.

"Are these all hotels?" Slater asked.

"Mostly, with some cantinas and shops in between."

The usual flock of young boys wasn't yet on duty along the road to beckon them toward the various establishments. Tourists didn't generally arrive this early. Pie de la Cuesta was popular mostly for its fabulous sunsets. Even then, it was Europeans more than Americans who ventured out here from the city. Whoever was after Slater wouldn't be likely to think of looking for him here.

"That's the place," she said, pointing to a low, long white building on the bay side of the road.

She'd stopped at Las Tres Marias on her first visit to Pie de la Cuesta. The attitude toward foreigners was generally polite but indifferent. Mostly Mexican families came here to eat at the open-air cantina with the immaculate, red-tiled patio floor. Of the small staff, only one woman at a serving window spoke enough English to be understood. Phoenix figured that any inquiries, even photographs, would be met with *"Yo no comprendo"* and a noncommittal shrug.

Slater parked in the sandy lot fronting the hotel patio. All that distinguished his Jeep from the other nondescript vehicles there was the top wrapped around the roll bar at the rear. Phoenix had packed her purchases into the colorful woven carry bags she'd bought at the market back in the city—everything they needed to look like just another pair of sun-seekers out here to relax and be left alone.

Between her meager Spanish and the halting English spoken by the woman at the serving window, Phoenix managed to get them a room. Slater stood guard meanwhile, squinting through his new dark glasses into the already bright sun along the vast, empty beach to one side of the hotel and the sandy road to the other. Phoenix might have told him he could relax out here so far from town, but she didn't. Maybe relaxing wasn't what Slater should do if he was to stay alive, and that was what she wanted more desperately than she had ever wanted anything in her life.

PORFIRO HAD DRIVEN PAST Las Tres Marias and parked in front of a small *tienda* further down the road and on the opposite side. He was surprised that the two Americanos knew about this out-of-the-way place, though he had observed her to be smart for a *gringa*. Smart or not, she wouldn't be likely to recognize Porfiro even if she looked straight at him. In his *campesino* clothes—loose white shirt and trousers, *huaraches* and straw hat—he bore little resemblance to the slicked-up tour driver she'd met at La Escarpadura.

Porfiro watched from across the road as the *gringa* arranged for a room. He picked up a broom and pretended to sweep the roadside as he made his observations. Even in his peasant disguise, Porfiro was wary of the eagle eye of the big guy, who was keeping a close lookout while she gestured and talked. Finally, the two of them followed a woman up a stairway into the hotel. Porfiro made his phone call then from a *cantina* next to the grocery where he'd parked the Chevy.

"Wait till they're out of the way, and take off with their car," the *gringo* Sax said over the phone. "I'll be out there soon. Wait for me at the turnoff to the highway."

Porfiro thought about protesting. He didn't want to get involved with stealing a car, though he'd done it before and he could hot-wire the rental Jeep fast. The patio at Las Tres Marias was just about deserted also, and even if somebody saw him they'd say nothing. He'd rather not do it all the same, but the money the mean *gringo* paid was good, more than enough to buy another Chevy if Porfiro couldn't get back here to pick up this one. The man on the phone was very bad, *un hombre muy malo*. Porfiro could tell that the first time he saw him.

"*No problema,*" Porfiro said. They were the words he knew *gringos* most loved to hear.

Chapter Twelve

Phoenix could hardly wait to get Slater out onto the beach. She knew it was wide-open there and maybe not the best place for a guy on the run. Still, he kept insisting they hadn't been followed, and he seemed to be well versed in such matters. Phoenix understood that, generally, there are only two types of people who specialize in that kind of knowledge—criminals and the police. She couldn't really picture Slater as the latter, and she didn't want to think any more right now about him being the former. She preferred the illusion that they were nothing more or less than a young couple who'd met on vacation in Mexico and were now spending a day at the beach.

"Beautiful, isn't it?" she called over the sound of the surf rolling in.

She'd put on the thong sandals, halter top and wrapped skirt she'd picked up at the street market. The filmy, printed skirt material swirled around her hips and caught between her legs in the stiff breeze that blew off the Pacific Ocean. Her sandals sank into the soft sand as she turned and ran back to Slater as fast as she could manage and threw her arms around his neck. His arms folded around her, and she pressed close to the solid wall of his chest. His fingers were in her hair, stroking, soothing. She knew she should be the one comforting him, but she didn't move. She let herself bask in the sheltering safety of his arms while the wind swirled around them and blew away all thoughts of anything but this perfect moment.

"We have to talk about what's really going on here," he began, but she covered his lips with her fingers.

"Not yet," she said. "Please, let us enjoy this beautiful place just a little longer."

He sighed and gave her a resigned smile. He kissed her fingers before she moved them away.

"Look who's here," he said.

He'd spoken too calmly to be referring to anyone dangerous, but Phoenix jumped back all the same with her heart beating suddenly fast. She breathed a deep sigh of relief to see a vendor approaching them. He was wearing the traditional Mexican loose, white shirt and trousers that were just right for a breezy day at the beach and a straw sombrero to protect his head against the hot sun. On his shoulder he balanced a shallow box.

"*¿Fruta fresca?*" he asked and lowered the box for Phoenix and Slater to see.

He was selling plastic cups filled with fruit—pineapple, citrus and melon in large, inviting chunks that looked as fresh as he proclaimed them to be. Phoenix could smell the pineapple, making her newly aware of how hungry she was. They never got the breakfast they'd been headed for earlier.

"I'll have two," she said eagerly.

Slater laughed. "Is that two just for you?"

"Yes," she said. "Two just for me."

Slater laughed again, and she was also newly aware of being hungry for that sound as well.

"*Cuatro, por favor,*" he said to the vendor.

Slater gave the vendor what looked like too many *pesos* and indicated that he didn't want change.

The vendor smiled wide. *"Muchas gracias,"* he said.

Phoenix could have told Slater this meant the vendor would be sending his colleagues around to plague *el americano rico* and that he probably would be back several times himself, but she didn't. Instead, she took her two cups of fruit and smiled just as widely herself.

"Let's sit down over there," she said, pointing toward the open-sided, thatch-roofed *palapas* nearby.

Weathered wooden beach chairs were lined up in the shade under the thatch. The sun was too hot to stand around in for very long, especially for Slater. His skin was a healthy, natural bronze-gold color, but he didn't yet have a base tan strong enough to tolerate the tropical sun. Phoenix could tell that he hadn't spent much time outdoors here in the daytime. She didn't care to think about what might have kept him inside except at night.

They'd reached the *palapas*. A short, stocky woman wearing an apron was beside them before they'd had time to sit down.

"Diez pesos," she said pointing at the chairs.

She meant that they had to rent the chairs for the day. She was carrying a towel and a small tray and most likely worked at Las Tres Marias. Phoenix was trying to put together enough fractured Spanish in her head to convey that she and Slater were guests at the hotel and the price of the chairs should go with that. Before she could formulate anything even close to that message, Slater had handed the woman a ten-*peso* note and three ones as a tip.

"We shouldn't have to pay to sit here," Phoenix said. "We're staying at the hotel."

The woman in the apron had already grabbed the money, said *"Gracias, señor,"* and was shuffling away.

"Cheap at twice the price," Slater said and settled into the chair with a sigh.

"You should at least have bargained with her," Phoenix said. "Five *pesos* would have been plenty."

"I don't feel like being anything but very agreeable at the moment," he said. "How's your fruit?"

"I haven't tasted it yet."

She put one cup down on the small, wooden table that Slater's *pesos* had apparently rented along with the chairs. A long, wooden toothpick was stuck in a piece of pineapple as an eating utensil. She took a bite of the juicy, fragrant fruit and was immediately as transfixed as Slater had been a while ago on the beach. She couldn't think of another flavor in the world to compare with the taste of this pineapple. The fruit she bought at her corner *bodega* back in Manhattan could hardly claim to be from the same plant family as this. The sweetness burst on her tongue so vividly that, for a moment, she couldn't bring herself to chew. Then, her hunger reminded her that her stomach was waiting none too patiently to be fed.

"This is good," Slater commented around a mouthful of his own.

Phoenix nodded. She was too busy gobbling the contents of first one cup, then the other, to speak. She'd emptied both before she turned to find Slater looking at her with a soft smile on his face. She was lifting the white paper napkin the vendor had given her to dab the juice from the corner of her mouth when Slater stopped her hand with his.

"Let me do that," he said.

He drew her toward him as he leaned over the space

between their beach chairs. Before she could prepare herself for his lips, they were on hers, but only for a second. He slid his tongue along her lower lip to the corner of her mouth and licked at the juice. The sensation aroused by that touch of the tip of his tongue to the sensitive corner of her mouth shot through her with a thrust as hot as the sun-baked sand. She couldn't stop the moan that rolled out of her throat. His tongue slipped back between her lips and across to the opposite corner of her mouth to lick there, too.

"Oh, no," she breathed against his lips, barely hearing what she'd said.

"Do you mean that?" he whispered as his mouth trailed downward to her chin then downward farther still onto her neck. "Do you want me to stop?" he murmured.

"No, please, no," she moaned. "Don't stop."

She felt his hands on her shoulders drawing her up out of her chair. His lips moved along her neck toward her ear, and she was grateful to have him holding her up because her knees had gone suddenly weak. His mouth reached her earlobe and nuzzled as he spoke.

"Let's go back to the room," he said.

Phoenix nodded once and leaned against him as his arm circled her waist and he guided her out from beneath the thatch and over the hot sand toward the rough wooden steps from the beach to the hotel patio. It occurred to her that they were wasting the ten *pesos* he'd paid for the chair rental. She let the thought drift away on the wind and the waves of her desire.

SLATER HAD WANTED TO swoop her up and carry her off the beach in his arms, but they were attracting enough attention already. He could see the lust burning in the eyes of the two Mexican men who were lounging on the patio drinking *cerveza*. Slater glared back at them until they looked away. He didn't intend to let any man look at Phoenix that way. She was for his eyes only.

Gazing down at her, he could understand why other men would want her. The white cloth of her halter top covered only part of the roundness of her breasts. The rest mounded golden and tempting and waiting to be touched. Any red-blooded man would be aroused just looking at her. Slater himself could resist the temptation only as far as the deserted stairwell. As they climbed the stairs, he pressed her against his side with one hand while the other reached for the bare skin above the waist of her skirt then roamed up over the white halter. His palm touched the hard bud of her nipple, and he heard himself moan the same way she had back on the beach.

"I can't keep my hands off you," he said in a voice so raspy he wondered if she could understand him.

They'd reached the top of the stairs. He walked faster, nearly stumbling in the intensity of his need to get her to their room and behind the closed door. She was clutching him around the waist and walking fast, too. He had to force himself to take his hand from the yielding firmness of her breasts in order to grope for the room key in the pocket of his pants. He fumbled for the lock while still holding her close.

"Hurry," she whispered.

She'd said that in a soft voice, but he heard the urgency there. She reached out and gripped the door handle.

"Let me help," she said.

He stuck the key into the lock and turned. She turned the knob at the same moment and pushed the door open. In the next second, they were over the threshold and she had shut the door behind them. Slater fumbled again to lock it with the key from the inside as was necessary in this old hotel. He barely had the lock turned before she was urging him toward the bed. He didn't bother to remove the key from the keyhole. His mind and his senses had already sped on to other things.

She was facing him now, only steps away from the bed. They'd both kicked off their beach sandals on the way from the door. His hands moved, as if by a will of their own, back to her breasts, fondling and stroking and pulling her toward him. He bent his knees and crouched slightly to align his hips to thrust forward against hers. She reached around him, and he felt her hands slide down his back to his buttocks. He registered a very pleasant surprise as she gripped him there and pulled him closer still. Her thighs parted, and he pressed between them.

Her body began to move sensuously, grinding against him, just as she'd done the other night on his patio. He thrilled, as he had then, at the passion of her response. He could hear her ragged breath as she murmured unintelligibly and he found her mouth with his. She rubbed her breasts against his palms, urging him to knead her flesh so hard he might have thought he was hurting her had it not been for the unmistakable sounds of pleasure she was making beneath his mouth. Phoenix was the most sensual woman he had ever known. She was more beautiful, more intoxicating, more unashamedly hungry to be loved by him than he'd ever thought it possible for a woman to be.

As if she'd heard that last thought of his, she pulled her mouth away from his and breathed, "Take me. Take me now."

He moved his hands, if only for a moment, from her

breasts and around her back to grab for the tie of her halter top and yank it loose. Her hands were moving also, pushing his tank shirt up his torso and over his head. He snatched the loosened halter from her body and froze for a moment. Her breasts were pale and flawless from her tan line down. Her nipples were rosy pink at their full circles and red at the tip. That redness pushed toward him in invitation.

Slater could do only one thing in response. He dropped to his knees and pulled her into his mouth, suckling one breast as he fondled the other. His tongue grazed her nipple. He marveled at its hardness, as hard as he was now beneath the beach slacks she'd bought for him at the marketplace. She put her hands behind his head to press him even more tightly to her breast. His teeth nipped her flesh, and she groaned. She moved one hand away from his head then, while the other continued to hold him close as his tongue tasted her.

Suddenly, her fingers were over his where he'd been touching her other breast. She pushed his hand down her body, over her bare skin to the band of her skirt, over her skirt and the small mound of her belly. She pushed his hand between their bodies where they were pressed hard together. She guided him to the cleft between her thighs and held his fingers beneath her own as she rocked her body back and forth. Then, she left his hand there to continue what she'd shown him she wanted. A moment later her fingers brushed the side of his face as he devoured her breast.

He had closed his eyes in concentration and ecstasy. He opened them now to see her touching herself, circling her nipple with her finger then grasping the full flesh and kneading it as he had done before. He heard her moan and glanced upward. Her mouth was open, and she was smiling in an expression of pure delight and desire. A flood crested inside Slater at that moment, and he could think of only one thing. He had to be inside her. He couldn't wait a single minute more.

The few articles of clothing they still had on fell away between them. He couldn't tell who took what off whom as they grappled together in mutual frenzy. Then, she was naked on the bed. He gazed down on her, aching at how unbelievably lovely she was. He could only allow himself a glance. He could feel her need was clamoring as wildly as his own. She opened her thighs, and he fitted himself between them and felt the moistness there.

He had no thoughts after that, except for one. When he had thrust inside her for the first time, he stopped dead still for a moment. In that instant, he knew that he had never felt anything like this before. The wet warmth of the most intimate part of her clutched him as closely as a glove and as perfectly fitted as if he'd been born to be there. He reveled in that perfection until her hips began to move beneath his, rising to meet him and press him still deeper inside her.

Slater pushed into her as she timed the rhythm of her hips exactly to his own. In what remained of his mind, he could see them moving together. With each thrust, she rose beneath him then drew him back into her each time he rocked away. Without words, she told him what she wanted from him, and all he cared about in the world was to give her that and much, much more.

At last, they reached the destination they had been rocketing toward. He heard her cry out, and he guessed he must have cried out, too, as he erupted into her. She stiffened, then let herself go. They pulsed together, their hips arched above the bed, for what must have been long minutes. Slater couldn't tell. He had gone beyond any sense of time or any sense of where he might be, to a place of pure sensation and, finally, of pure peace. Phoenix sighed in his arms, and he knew she must be in that place, too.

"UP IN THE ROOM," Porfiro said to Sax and gestured toward the second floor of Las Tres Marias Hotel. "They went for a walk on the beach, then upstairs."

"*Siesta* time," Sax said with a lewd laugh that made plain what he was thinking.

Porfiro had met Sax at the highway junction as planned. Now, they were back at the hotel leaning against the *hombre* McCain's Jeep. Porfiro looked away, off down the dusty road. He didn't like this Sax at all. Porfiro was sorry to say that he probably liked Sax even less than he liked the big guy over in the hotel. That *hombre* might play the bull and push his weight around, but this Sax was a snake. Porfiro would prefer a bull to a snake any day.

"You take a break now," Sax was saying. He shoved some bills into Porfiro's hand. "Get yourself something to eat in the cantina while I size up the situation here. Then you can take this wreck of his back to town for me. I'll pay you more tonight at the Esperanza Club."

Porfiro counted several fifty-*peso* notes in his hand. He nodded, then headed for the cantina. He was thinking how the only thing good about this Sax *hombre* was his money.

Meanwhile, Sax had slipped behind the Jeep, ready to slide under the chassis just long enough to do what had to be done.

Chapter Thirteen

Phoenix had been lazily, luxuriously half awake for quite some time before the phone rang.

"Let me talk to McCain."

The man's voice sounded familiar to her but distant in memory like someone she might have heard on television or radio. Phoenix covered the receiver and shook Slater's shoulder. His skin was warm and smooth to touch, but she had already begun to feel a chill as she wondered how the man on the phone could have known they were here at Pie de la Cuesta.

"Slater, someone wants to talk to you."

He moaned and rolled toward here, reaching for her bare thigh under the damp, rumpled sheet.

"What?" he said with a yawn.

"There's a man on the phone for you."

Slater bolted straight upright grabbing for the nightstand then looking almost frantically around the room. Phoenix guessed what he was after.

"I put your gun over on the dresser," she said.

She'd done that some time earlier, on her way to the bathroom. She hadn't been with Slater long enough to get used to the fact that he slept with a loaded firearm within reach. The thought of that made her very nervous.

What if he had a violent dream and mistook it for reality? She was beginning to wonder if his life might not be a violent dream in general. That possibility all but destroyed the romantic reverie she'd been drifting through before the phone rang. Which reminded her…

"Slater. The phone."

"I know."

He took the receiver from her hand. The softness in his face, which she remembered from earlier on the beach, was gone now, replaced by hard angles and tension.

"Who is this?" he barked into the phone without the nicety of a greeting.

He listened a moment, then barked again. "Where are you?"

Slater must not have liked the answer to that because he leapt out of bed with a scowl on his face. Phoenix still couldn't help noticing how gorgeous he looked standing there nude in the shaded light from the half-open blinds. Mostly, however, his agitation frightened her.

"What do you mean you're here?" he growled into the phone.

He covered the receiver and growled at her as well. "Get the key out of the lock."

He gestured at the door. Phoenix hesitated only a second before jumping out of bed herself. She pulled the sheet with her, wrapping it around her body. She could sense that this wasn't the time to be naked and vulnerable. She hurried to the door, but the keyhole was empty.

"It's gone," she said. How could that be? She looked around on the floor but found nothing.

"You've been up here, haven't you?" Slater shouted into the phone. "You stole the room key."

He gestured toward his pants which were just out of reach on the floor. Phoenix picked them up and tossed them to him. She was already struggling as fast as she could into her own underwear.

"Slater, what's going on?" she asked.

He made a warning gesture as if to silence her.

"I want to know what is going on," she said again.

Phoenix grabbed for the skirt she'd worn earlier then discarded it. Instinct told her something more substantial than that gauzy garment might be in order now. She hurried to the tote bag she'd left on a chair and rummaged for a pair of a shorts. It was still too much the hot part of the day for long pants. What she really wanted, of course, was some answers. Slater didn't appear inclined to provide any. He'd turned his back to her as he pulled on his pants with one hand while the other clutched the receiver so hard his knuckles were white.

"You stay away from this room," he was saying into the phone in the most menacing tone she'd ever heard him use.

"Who's coming up here?" she asked as he slammed the receiver back into the carriage.

Phoenix scrambled into her shorts and pulled on the T-shirt she'd been wearing when they first arrived here. Slater pulled on the loose-fitting tropical print shirt she had bought for him at the market this morning. He grabbed his gun from the dresser. Phoenix had no experience with guns—in fact, she hated them—but she thought he was checking to make sure it was loaded.

She was dressed except for her shoes, but what should she do now? The glow of lovemaking, which had been so much with her when she first awoke, had totally dissipated now.

Slater cursed under his breath.

"What's going on here?" she demanded yet again. "I want to know."

"We were followed after all."

"Who followed us, and how did he get the key?"

Slater waved toward the door. "He snuck up here when we were asleep, poked the key out of the lock, then fished it through the crack under the door. It's an old trick."

She gasped. Maybe this kind of thing was an old trick to Slater, but not to her. "He could have been up here when we were..." she trailed off, looking toward the bed.

They'd been making so much noise while they were making love that they would never have heard someone at the door. Phoenix felt herself blush despite the circumstances. Slater only nodded and hurried to the window which looked down on the parking area at the road side of the hotel.

"Damn," he said. "The Jeep is gone."

"Somebody stole your Jeep?"

"I'm going down to the beach to take care of this guy," Slater said. "You stay here."

"I'm not staying anywhere, especially not if somebody's wandering around with the key."

Slater grabbed her shoulders before she'd finished speaking. He gripped her so hard it hurt. She tried to pull away but couldn't.

"Listen to me," he barked in just about the same tone he'd used with the man on the phone. "This is a very dangerous man we're dealing with. You should know that. I want you to stay here."

Why should she know how dangerous he was? She didn't know anything...except one thing. Slater had let go of her and was on his way to the door. She raced ahead of him and blocked his path.

"Don't go," she said. "We'll call the police."

He stared at her.

"I know getting the police involved could mean trouble, but anything's better than having you get hurt."

She meant that more than any words she'd ever spoken in her life. She said it with passion. Slater must have been affected by that because he took her face in his hands. He looked deep into her eyes for a moment then kissed her on the mouth hard but not for long.

"Don't worry. I won't get hurt," he said, pulling away. "Now, I have to go."

Moving his hands from her face to her upper arms, he picked her up off the floor as easily as if she were a rag doll. He lifted her away from the door then set her back down. He had the door open and was out into the hallway before she could make a move to stop him.

"Stay here," he said once again as he shut the door behind him.

Phoenix knew that staying here while Slater went out to face danger alone was the one thing she couldn't do.

SHE'D ACTUALLY SAID they should call in the police, and Slater could tell she'd meant that, too. He knew he should be concentrating on Sax and nothing else right now, but he couldn't help thinking about what Phoenix had said back in the room. She really did care for him after all, enough to put herself in possible danger of going to prison to keep him safe. From that moment on, Slater knew he would do everything in his power to save her from that fate. Until today, his first loyalty had always been to his badge, but that had changed. Nothing was more important than Phoenix now.

Sax had said they should meet on the beach, but Slater was alert to a possible trick of some kind such as an ambush before he could get to the beach. He edged down the stairway with his back to the wall and his gun out. When he reached the bottom he lowered the weapon to his side where it was less noticeable but still at the ready. He didn't want to cause a panic or to prompt the hotel staff to come after him. He was certain some of them would be armed. This was Mexico after all, and this little *cantina* was most likely beyond the reach of the Acapulco city police. Proprietors of places like this small hotel had to be prepared for trouble. He didn't want them to think of him as that. While he was explaining himself, Phoenix would be on her own with Sax in the vicinity, and he couldn't let that happen.

Slater peered out from the bottom of the stairway, first to one side of the opening to the patio, then to the other. Sax was nowhere in sight. The two men who'd been drinking beer earlier were gone. A tourist family with three children filled one of the red Formica-topped tables. The mother studied the all-in-Spanish menu with a perplexed expression on her face while her husband glanced furtively around as if he might be wondering how he'd managed to take such an obviously wrong turn off the beaten path. The children began to squabble among themselves, and their parents turned their attention to that. Slater used their preoccupied moment to slip past without being noticed. He'd checked out the parking lot from the doorway. There was no vehicle he would guess to belong to Sax, who probably wouldn't be seen in a car as old as any of these. Slater also noted that his own rental Jeep was still nowhere to be found.

He palmed the pistol and slid it halfway into the pocket of his pants where it could be hidden by the tail

of the boxy, bright-patterned shirt he had pulled on upstairs but hadn't taken time to button. As his feet hit the
beach at the bottom of the steps, Slater was glad he *had*
bothered to grab his sandals. The burning hot midday
had passed, but that didn't mean the beach had begun to
cool. He could feel the scorching sand radiating heat
through his sandal soles. It occurred to Slater that he
must look like a refugee from an Hawaiian golf tour-
nament in this outfit, but he didn't have time to care
about appearances now.

Slater kept to the high side of the beach closest to the
hotels where a low wall offered some potential cover.
He could hop over it if he had to, provided there was
time to do that before the bullets started to fly. He was
a few yards along that wall, and he still hadn't spotted
Sax. In the other direction, the beach was nearly deserted
except for a few strollers at the edge of the surf. Slater
could tell that none of them were Sax. He had to be
along this stretch of sand before Slater, if he was really
out here at all. Slater had a scary thought. What if Sax
had lured Slater away from the hotel in order to get to
Phoenix? She was back there now, alone in the room.
Slater stopped in his tracks, clutching the gun in his
pocket. He glanced back at the hotel shining white in
the sun, then down the beach ahead. That was when he
saw what he'd been looking for.

The sun was so bright Slater had trouble making out
details against the glare. Sunglasses were the one thing
he had forgotten to bring with him from the room. Still,
the man in the beach chair at the far end of the same
thatched *palapas* where Slater and Phoenix had been sitting earlier couldn't be anyone other than SideMan Sax.
Who else would be out here on the beach in this heat
with a suit on? As Slater eased closer, he could see it

was a white suit, no doubt SideMan's concession to the tropics and not purchased at the street market like Slater's getup, he would guess. Fortunately, this wasn't a fashion competition. He and Sax were here to duke it out over much more crucial territory than that.

If Sax thought of any of this as crucial, he definitely wasn't letting it show. He'd slid his skinny body into lounge position deep in the old wooden chair with his legs stretched out straight in front of him and his feet propped on one of the rickety square tables that went with the chairs. His polished wing tips had been replaced by woven Mexican sandals much classier than Slater's rubber-soled ones. Sax was a cool customer all right. He leaned back in the chair with his dark glasses perched on his nose, staring out to sea. Maybe he'd already checked Slater out on his way from the hotel and knew where he was even now. Sax would know Slater wasn't likely to start any gunplay out here. He and Sax were alone on this stretch of beach for now, and that was the way Slater wanted it. There'd be no innocent bystanders to worry about, nobody to keep him from focusing full attention on what he had in mind. Slater pulled the gun out of his pocket as he approached Sax's chair.

"You don't need your piece," Sax said in a drawling voice that betrayed little interest in what was going on.

"You must have eyes in the side of your head," Slater said. "I hear that's true of a lot of snakes."

He hadn't put the gun away even though it was fully visible now. His open shirt was flapping in the breeze and wouldn't hide anything.

"If you're trying to get my back up, you can forget it. That kinda cheap trick stuff don't work with me."

"I can see you're just kicking back out here enjoying the scenery," Slater said.

He'd moved between the chairs one down from where Sax was sitting and positioned himself with his back to the sun. Sax had the visual disadvantage this way.

"I'm not enjoying anything about this dump," Sax said with the old sneer in his voice. "Scrawny dogs and peddlers. That's all you see here."

"Maybe you haven't been looking in the right places."

Sax pulled his feet off the wooden table and sat forward in his chair, straightening the lapels of his white suit jacket over the white polo shirt he had on. The shirt was buttoned all the way to his neck which made Slater wonder if this guy had any blood in his veins for the sun to heat up. Sax stood slowly and brushed off the back of his trousers with his hand. He walked around the table and took a stance on the ocean side of Slater.

"Maybe I shoulda been lookin' where you had your eyes lately," Sax drawled. "Up that Farraday broad's skirt."

Slater knew it was a challenge the minute he heard it. Maybe he knew that's what it would be even before Sax opened his slimy mouth. Slater would have loved to stick his gun in this guy's ear and give him the kind of scare he was asking for. On the other hand, the part of Slater that was still more cop than man with a woman under his skin needed to find out exactly what Sax had in mind. Besides, eventually, Slater would be looking for more of a showdown with this creep than a gun in his ear could give.

"If you hate it so much here, why'd you come?" Slater asked.

"I've been keeping my eye on you, and I don't like what I see."

"How's that?"

"You've been draggin' your heels since day one, and now I see why. You've gone sweet on the chick."

Slater clenched his jaw to keep himself from saying what he thought about hearing this piece of trash talk that way about Phoenix.

"Good thing I am here," Sax added. "I'll be takin' over now. I've got a feeling I can find out what Laurent wants to know. Maybe I'll go up to that room of yours and get down to some interrogating right now."

Sax's sneer was wreaking havoc with Slater's self-control.

"You stay away from her," he said, taking a deliberately menacing step toward Sax and glaring into his smirking face.

"You lookin' for a piece of me?" Sax taunted.

He was backing away from Slater now, beckoning him to follow.

"I don't want just a piece of you, Sax," Slater growled. "I'd like to sweep up this beach with the whole *enchilada.*"

Sax threw back his skinny neck and laughed. A silver tooth glinting in the front of his mouth caught Slater's attention and seemed to ignite his temper with its flash of reflected sun. He took his first swing then, but he didn't have the kind of sure footing he needed to connect. His size and weight made the sand shift beneath his feet. Sax feinted away and continued to back off toward the surf. He probably had a weapon on him somewhere, but he'd made no move to grab for it yet.

"I don't blame you for bringin' her out here," he said with his snake smile on his face. "This is just the kind of no-tell hotel where I'd take a lying, thieving tramp like her."

Slater understood that these words were intended to

send him even further out of control. He told himself that wasn't happening. Still, staying in control didn't mean he couldn't beat the crap out of this jerk. Slater lunged forward and grabbed Sax's arm, squeezing and twisting hard. Sax must have learned some martial arts in his shady past because he made a quick, deft turn out of Slater's grip. Sax reached behind him, but Slater was too fast for him. He struck Sax's arm hard just as he was pulling his weapon from the back of his waistband. The gun spun from his grip and buried itself in the sand several feel away.

They had been moving steadily down the beach toward the water. Sax couldn't get back to the hotel side of the sand without going over Slater. Sax turned and, to Slater's surprise, ran into the surf. Slater followed. As soon as he did, he realized why Sax had made this move. The sand shifted beneath Slater's considerable weight, making him stumble as he trailed Sax into the moving water. Slater could feel the undertow already, even before he was in up to his knees. Sax bounced along ahead, just out of reach. His skinny, lightweight frame was an advantage out here.

Slater would have been wise to get back to the beach, pull his piece and force Sax onto dry land at gunpoint. Maybe Slater had lost control after all because, at the moment, he couldn't have cared less what was or wasn't wise. All he cared about was getting his hands on Sax and wringing his scrawny neck. That thought consumed Slater's mind and filled his heart, so much so that he failed to notice the breaker rolling in to smack him hard just above the knees and pull the sand out from under his feet.

Chapter Fourteen

Phoenix saw them and broke into a run. She'd thought they weren't out here at first. The sand was empty except for two Mexican boys on horses—one dappled, one chestnut—moving slowly way off down the beach. She was about to head back to the hotel when her brain registered that the two boys were pointing and gesturing toward the sea. She let her gaze follow those gestures and saw the two men grappling there. She might not have recognized Slater if it hadn't been for his size. His hair was plastered flat and streaming. His shirt was pulled halfway off and soaking. He was struggling to keep upright as the other man leapt on top of him, trying to force him down into the water. She could almost feel the exhaustion in Slater's legs as the current pulled against him. She'd been out in that surf on her previous trips to Pie de la Cuesta. She knew how powerful the undertow was here, and they were out farther than she'd ever dared to venture. She could tell that their grapplings were gradually carrying them out farther still.

"Come back, Slater," she cried.

The wind carried her words off with it. Slater would never be able to hear her, but maybe that was best. He needed to concentrate on keeping his head above water.

Any distraction might prove fatal. That far out, with somebody holding his head submerged and the current pulling him down as well, Slater might drown.

Phoenix gasped at the thought. She was into the surf herself now with the foam lapping against her bare legs. She could feel the force of the tide pull already, sliding the silt away beneath her feet, buckling her knees so she had to step backward to keep from falling. She wanted to rush to Slater's aid, but she knew she couldn't make it. She was a good swimmer, but not strong enough to get to him in this riptide current that all the guidebooks warned against. Apparently, Slater and whoever he was wrestling with hadn't read those warnings. Phoenix watched, feeling helpless, as the two men bobbed and staggered beyond her reach.

She had to do something. She'd guessed that Slater's opponent in the surf was probably the same man who'd been on the phone earlier and maybe the person who shot at him that morning as well. That meant, if Slater made it to the beach, he'd still have to get away from here. Phoenix headed out of the water, scolding herself for thinking in terms of *if* Slater got back to the beach instead of *when*. She scrambled as fast as she could through the sand. She'd lost one sandal to the surf, and the beach was scorching. She didn't care. She just kept on scrambling.

"*Muchachos,*" she cried against the wind. "*Muchachos, vamos aguí.*"

She suspected her Spanish was wrong. She couldn't remember the correct way to say "Come here" at the moment. She'd captured the attention of the two boys on horseback anyway. They were looking curiously in her direction. Then, one of them picked up his reins as if he might be getting ready to ride away. They were both riding bareback using rope bits as halters. She must look like she was trying to run them down. She couldn't let them get away.

"*Tengo dinero,*" she cried, groping in the pocket of her shorts.

She'd had her money in there when she was shopping at the street market earlier. Fortunately, that money hadn't fallen out or the credit and bank cards either. She understood that these boys would only respond to cash.

"*Tengo mucho dinero para sus caballos,*" she shouted.

She was amazed and grateful that the Spanish words she needed had managed to appear on her lips at just the right moment, like a miracle. The boys urged their horses toward her as she stumbled across the sand.

SLATER HAD NEVER RUN from a fight in his life, but if he could get himself free long enough that was exactly what he intended to do this time. He'd gotten himself into this situation by not listening to his head. He had to make up for that now.

Slater grasped Sax's throat in what might have been a choke hold had he been able to get a grip and keep it. Slater spluttered and wheezed as his mouth and nose filled with salty water. The choke hold hadn't worked. He'd have to try something else. He charged upward to gulp a full breath of air before suddenly releasing his resistance and allowing himself to be pushed beneath the surface. Sax must have been startled by the change because he toppled off balance.

Slater felt Sax's hold loosen. This was an opportunity that might not present itself again. Slater dove the short distance to the bottom, grabbed a fistful of the coarse sand there and headed back toward the light above. He broke the surface with a plunge and found Sax in mid-turn as if he might have been trying to figure out where Slater went. He grabbed Sax's arm and flung the fistful of sand directly into his eyes. Sax clawed at his face while struggling to keep afloat.

Again, Slater recognized a moment of opportunity. He let go of Sax and struck out toward the shore. He hadn't done much swimming outside of pools. The long, smooth strokes that worked well there weren't so easy here. He had to arc his arm high and chop it down through the surface in a hard plunge in order to achieve the power he needed to move forward. All the while he was doing this, the force of the rushing tide drew backward beneath the surface of the water, trying to tow him out into its depths. The wave breaking beachward over his head and propelling him with it provided only an instant of relief from the ocean's pull. He could almost hear the call of water witches and demons of the deep beckoning him to come and sleep with them. That illusion urged him on.

He had used up much of his energy in his grappling with Sax. Slater knew too well how little stamina remained for battling the sea. He gulped ragged mouthfuls of air as he thrust his face upward then ducked back underwater where he held his breath until his lungs nearly burst while he stroked with what strength he had left. His throat burned from the briny water he had swallowed and grated from the sand that mixed with the swirling sea. His eyes stung even when he squeezed them shut. He opened them on his next upward lunge for breath and saw the shoreline ahead, maybe not so far off but still what felt like lifetimes away.

Slater understood that it would be wise to swim parallel to the shore for a while in search of a break in the waves before making for land. He didn't have enough steam left for that, and he knew it. He was weakening fast. In a matter of minutes, he would be beyond hope. His arms and legs would cease to be a match for the power of nature, and he would be carried outward then down to the home of those beckoning voices he'd imagined a moment ago.

The temptation was great to let go now, to drop his aching arms to his sides, to stop gasping and gulping and allow himself to slide into what would very soon become a simple peace. He acknowledged what a relief that would be at the same second his sea-sodden brain recognized what it had been thinking. His body plunged forward then, as if spurred by a will beyond thought. He wanted to live. He had to live, and to do that he must fight harder than he had ever fought before.

His muscles responded with a charge that could only have come from his heart, as Slater called upon resources he'd never known he possessed. His arms lifted through the pain of overtaxed sinews and beyond the thrash through the water. His legs pumped as if he were running for his life, which of course he was. He gulped air and sand and spray then submerged again to focus all that was in him on the thrashing and pumping. With every ounce of strength and courage he could muster, Slater willed himself under the breakers and through the backward tow in one last, mighty stretch toward land.

Then, in the final possible moment, when he was certain he could not lift his arm one more time through the strain and pull he'd already inflicted upon his tortured shoulder muscles, he was in the shallows. His feet found the bottom, and he staggered forward. He tried to come upright, but he couldn't manage it. Doubled over and stumbling, Slater lurched toward the beach as his lungs coughed up sea and sand. His eyes were too ravaged by saltwater to open more than a slit without burning pain. He could allow himself only an instant's glimpse of sunlight shimmering on shallow waves before his eyelids clamped shut against the brightness. He was stumbling, falling and rising again, half blind when hands touched his arm.

Pain leapt through his shoulder as if he'd been prodded by molten steel, and he tried to cry out. He could tell he had torn the muscles there so badly that they would be a long time mending, but he didn't care. He had reached the shore, and he was alive. His eyes streamed sea water and tears, and his throat rasped toward a cry of joy he couldn't yet utter. He dropped upon the sand and rolled over onto his back, almost oblivious to the aching agony in almost every part of his body.

Slater thought he heard his name being called through the rushing ocean roar that still filled his ears. For a moment, he thought he was being revisited by those sea witches he'd imagined. As his eyelids fluttered open just enough to take in the apparition leaning over him, he understood that another spirit altogether was beckoning him now. She'd been calling him all along though he hadn't comprehended that until this moment. Hers had been the voice which summoned that last surge of will to pound through the waves past endurance so he might save his life and be with her.

"Phoenix," he whispered without sound.

"SLATER," SHE CRIED. "You have to get up. We have to get out of here."

She dragged at his arms, and he groaned. Phoenix shielded her eyes with her hand and squinted against the sun as she gazed out to sea. She couldn't see anyone there. Had Slater drowned the man he'd been fighting with? Was he a murderer now in addition to whatever other crimes he had committed? She was shocked to realize how much this possibility made her want to shield him against discovery the same way she was protecting her eyes from the glare. She dragged harder on his arm. He groaned more loudly still, but he stirred this time.

"You have to stand up," she said. "I've figured out how we can get away from here."

Slater croaked a sound too rasping for her to understand.

"What did you say?" she asked.

Two beach vendors were standing nearby watching. One of them, a woman in a brightly multicolored skirt and white blouse, came forward now. She was selling cans of soft drinks from a flat, wooden box she carried on her head. She held out a can to Phoenix, a brand of cola she'd never heard of before. She'd salvaged a few *pesos* from her transaction with the boys. Phoenix dug in her pocket for the money, but the vendor woman shook her head.

"No necesita pagar," she said. "For him."

She gestured toward Slater, and Phoenix was even more startled by the words of English than by the offer of help.

"Gracias," she said and took the can.

The woman had already popped the top open. Phoenix knelt down beside Slater and held the can to his lips. He didn't open his mouth at first, and the liquid ran over his chin. That seemed to rouse him, and he took a gulp that Phoenix could tell was too much too soon. He choked, and she moved the can away.

"More," he rasped.

She'd understood that clearly and returned the can to his lips. He drank several mouthfuls but more slowly this time. He pushed himself up on one elbow from the sand. She could tell by the grimace on his face that it hurt him to move, especially to use his arms for support. She helped him as best she could to move into a sitting position on the sand. His shirt had been torn off in the water, and he had lost his sandals. He was wearing his wet trousers, and that was all.

"Have to get away," he rasped again, even more clearly now.

Phoenix felt a touch on her elbow. She spun around, half expecting to see Slater's adversary from the sea looming over her. Instead, it was the same vendor woman who'd given Slater the can of cola. She had another woman at her side now.

"*Mi amiga,*" the woman said, indicating her companion who was carrying a huge pile of T-shirts over one arm. A long, white canvas bag hung by a rope cord from her other shoulder.

The woman took a T-shirt from her friend's pile and held it out to Phoenix.

"*Para el señor,*" the woman said.

Phoenix looked from the cola vendor to her friend who was smiling shyly. Phoenix could see the compassion in that smile. These women were poor and understood what it was to have trouble and to need help. Phoenix took the shirt.

"*Muchas gracias,*" she said returning the smile. "Thank you so much."

Meanwhile, Slater had pulled himself upright. Phoenix handed him the T-shirt. He tried to put it on, but he could only raise his arms barely level with his shoulders, no higher. He groaned in agony just getting them that far. Phoenix had to ease the shirt up his arms and over his head.

"*¡Andando!*"

One of the boys who owned the horses had run up to Phoenix's side and was motioning her to hurry.

"*¡Mira!*" he said with agitation in his voice.

He was tugging at her arm and motioning out to sea. Phoenix shielded her eyes again but couldn't see what the boy was pointing at. The sun was too strong to make out anything but sparkles as bright as a mass of light-bulbs on the rippling surface of the water beyond the breakers. Then she saw it, a head bobbing along parallel to the beach and headed back in the direction of Las Tres Marias. She was sure that head belonged to the man Slater had been struggling with in the waves.

"We have to get out of here right now," she said to Slater.

He had already managed to pull himself halfway to his feet. She put her shoulder under his arm and helped him straighten further. The boy who had told them to hurry took Slater's other side, and the three of them began moving laboriously over the sand.

"Where are we going?" Slater asked, still in a rough whisper.

"I've arranged a ride for us," Phoenix said.

"A ride?" Slater still sounded a little dazed.

"Your charger, my knight," Phoenix couldn't resist saying as they approached the two rather swaybacked mares and the second Mexican boy who was holding them by their rope halters.

"*Mi caballo,*" said the other boy, who'd been helping Phoenix half drag Slater up the beach.

Slater stared at the horses then at Phoenix in what looked like disbelief.

"I found out that there's a bus back into Acapulco," she said.

"*Sí. El autobus*," the boy said, gesturing ahead toward the row of hotels and the road beyond.

"All we have to do is get back to the highway," Phoenix said.

"On these?"

Slater looked skeptically at the old ponies.

"These cost me just about every penny I had on me," Phoenix said, "and we have to hurry."

"*Sí, andando,*" the boy said, agreeing with Phoenix's concern that they make tracks *pronto.*

Getting Slater onto the back of the chestnut mare required the combined effort of Phoenix and both young boys. She could tell from the sharpness of Slater's moans that he had seriously damaged his shoulder muscles in his life-or-death sprint through the waves. She wondered if he would need a doctor and where they could get one. She'd have to work all of that out later. Right now, they needed to escape back to town. Pie de la Cuesta was not the refuge she'd hoped for after all. Still, she looked wistfully back up the white sand toward the small hotel where she and Slater had made such wonderful love what unfortunately now felt like ages ago. Phoenix sighed as she gathered up the reins of the dappled horse she'd just mounted and prepared to urge her away from Las Tres Marias and toward the next pathway to the road.

"*Señorita.*"

It was the cola vendor again. She was tugging at Phoenix's leg and handing up two pairs of *huaraches* that looked like they would be just about Phoenix and Slater's sizes. Once more, Phoenix felt tears moisten her lashes. She couldn't remember when she had ever experienced such generosity or when she had ever needed it more.

"Gracias," she said.

She wished she possessed the Spanish vocabulary to say more, but there was no time anyway. The two Mexican boys were already tugging the ponies by their rope halters away from the small group of vendors that had gathered and up the beach in the opposite direction from the sea.

"Vaya con Dios," said the cola vendor and her friend together.

"Vaya con Dios," echoed the other vendors.

Phoenix raised her hand in grateful farewell and prayed that she and Slater would, in fact, "Go with God" wherever they might be headed.

Chapter Fifteen

Slater could hardly believe how much his body ached. All the time they were dragging him up onto this broken-down nag, he was whispering to himself, "I can do this. I can do this." The problem was that he *had* to do this, and he wasn't thinking about just keeping himself from falling off the horse as he trotted and then slowly galloped over the sand. The really hard thing Slater had to do was to make sure Phoenix stayed safe from SideMan Sax and the methods he'd hinted at for making her talk. Sax was pure thug through and through. He got a kick out of hurting people. He'd seen the glint in Sax's eyes, stiletto sharp and made of the same cold steel. This guy was fierce in pursuit of his target, and he was after Phoenix now. He only cared about taking Slater down so he could get to her, and maybe also because he got a kick out of that, too.

Slater had run into twisted types like Sax before.

A cop can't help but do that. Slater had learned long ago to take these characters in his stride, but all of that was out the window now. Slater took Sax's pursuit of Phoenix very personally. Slater not only wanted Sax off the planet, he intended to put him there. The only hitch was that Slater was still a man with a badge, even when undercover work kept him from carrying it in his pocket. His assignment was to catch Beldon Laurent with dirt on his hands, or to produce the information that would help somebody else prove that dirt was there. Slater still hoped he could fulfill this assignment and keep Phoenix safe at the same time. That meant he had to avoid a final showdown with Sax for a while longer and get Phoenix back to Acapulco.

For now, Slater was making this ride along the beach slumped over the neck of the horse. Sitting upright would have been too painful to bear. Phoenix galloped on ahead with the wind in her hair. Slater picked his head up from the horse's mane far enough to gaze at her for a moment. She looked so beautiful in the sunlight that the sight hurt his eyes, but not in the way the sand and saltwater had done. This ache went straight to his heart. He could imagine nothing better than to keep gazing at her forever. He could also imagine nothing worse than having that vision interrupted by a prison sentence or worse. The pang of that possibility carried fear with it like poison on a dagger's point. Slater slumped back down again and kneed his pony to a faster pace.

They left the pathway from the beach to the road and clomped along the shoulder in the direction of the highway junction. Phoenix was out in front still and seemed to know where she was going and what they had to do when they got there. Slater had been vaguely aware of her conferring with the two Mexican kids back on the beach, something about tying the horses up at the junction. He'd been too preoccupied with the pain in his body at that moment to pick up on the exact details. He was almost accustomed to that pain by now, as if his muscles had always burned as if his limbs were about to fall off. He'd begun to wonder what Phoenix's plan might be. Had he heard somebody mention a bus?

Slater lifted his head to look over his shoulder and back along the road. His nerve endings responded immediately to the twisting movement, sending a shock of pain down his arm and across his shoulders. Slater groaned but held the position long enough to make sure SideMan wasn't behind them. The road was clear except for a couple of dusty, old cars lumbering along, neither moving fast enough to be in pursuit of anything more than a leisurely trip from one *cantina* to another.

Slater turned painfully back toward the road ahead. They were approaching the crossroads, and Phoenix was slowing her horse. Slater took a deep breath and straightened up far enough to pull in on the reins and bring his horse to a slow trot. Slater forced himself to sit up straighter still. He would have sworn he could feel each vertebra grind against the next. He gritted his teeth and pulled himself as upright as he could manage. His aching shoulders slumped forward, and his neck refused to hold his head straight up just yet. Still, he was no longer slumped over his horse and hanging on for dear life. For now, Slater considered that a major accomplishment.

By the time they reached the junction, he had even convinced himself he was ready to swing his leg over the horse and slide off. The chestnut trotted up next to Phoenix's motley mare as if on cue. Phoenix was on the ground by then, holding her horse and Slater's while he braced himself to dismount. "Just do it," he told himself silently. He sucked in another deep breath and started counting in his head to distract himself from what he was about to feel. He was almost to ten when the groan escaped, but he'd made it to the ground in the meantime. His knees threatened to buckle under him, but he didn't let them. He could tell from the expression on Phoenix's face just how much agony he must appear to be in.

"Can you make it?" she asked.

Slater nodded, though the discomfort caused by even that small movement made him wonder if he could actually perform what his nod promised. He reminded himself that he had no choice. Phoenix walked both horses to a nearby signpost and tethered them there. Slater forced his spine straight and plastered what he hoped was a smile on his face for her to see as she hurried back to him. He couldn't square his shoulders no matter how hard and painfully he tried.

"What now?" he asked, pleased to hear that his voice could work itself past his still-ravaged throat.

"We're supposed to stand over there."

Phoenix pointed toward the highway. She'd taken Slater's arm and was urging him in that direction. He willed himself to follow though his legs felt as if they weighed a ton each.

"Those boys on the beach told me we could catch a bus back to town here. They said there's several of them running along the highway this time of day. I hope they were right about that."

Slater heard the anxiety in her voice. He looked back down the dusty road they'd just left. No SideMan in sight yet, but he'd be coming before long. Slater was sure that SideMan would have a car, too. He was probably on the way to wherever he'd left it now. Unfortunately, there was little chance he'd drowned in the surf. A snake like Sax was never gotten rid of that easily.

"Thank heaven," Phoenix breathed.

Slater guessed what the words meant even before he turned around to see a bus coming down the highway toward them. He whispered a prayerful thanks of his own, but that was before he registered the details of the bizarre contraption approaching them. The vehicle was designed like a yellow school bus, painted blue and white, but that was where the resemblance ended. It was probably the oldest bus Slater had ever seen still running. It was dented all over, and the paint was chipped and marred. The bulk of the body swayed low toward the shoulder on the right, as if the suspension on that side must be completely shot. The sign on the front said Coyuca even though the sign Slater noticed at the side of the road indicated the bus was actually headed for Acapulco now.

The windows were what made this rundown hulk truly bizarre. The top half of the front window had been shielded to keep the bright tropical sun out of the driver's eyes. Dark blue velvet cloth had been stretched across the wide glass. Tassels with blue velvet balls on them fringed the fabric and bounced crazily as the bus bumped over the uneven road. The top half of all the side windows had been covered by a thick layer of paint. As the ancient vehicle pulled to a stop in response to Phoenix's frantic waving, Slater noticed that the window paint had been decorated with carefully etched line drawings of stars and half moons and sun shapes with rays bursting around them.

Slater stared at those designs for a moment. Someone had taken great care to try to make this old wreck just a little bit beautiful. For some reason, Slater found that thought encouraging. He stepped up behind Phoenix almost with the confidence that this rattling heap could get them back to town in one piece. That, of course, wouldn't guarantee that his aching body could survive the ride.

THE BUS WAS CROWDED with Mexicans, some sitting three to a seat designed for two. The passengers stared at Phoenix and Slater as they lurched down the aisle toward the back of the already moving bus. Phoenix had noticed, during her stay here in Mexico, how polite and unintrusive the people generally were. She couldn't blame them for being less so now. She'd guess they hadn't seen too many *norteamericanos* on this bus before today.

She and Slater weren't looking their best, either. They both wore a coating of dust on their legs from the gallop over the beach and down the road. Slater was especially disheveled. His hair had sprung into wild waves from drying in the wind. His trousers, in addition to their dusting of road dirt, were stiff from the salt of the sea water. He was walking strangely too, with a lopsided shambling gait that told her he must be hurting badly. The other passengers must have noticed that because they had the same sympathetic look in their eyes that Phoenix had noticed from the vendors on the beach.

Probably in response to that sympathy, a man in the second row from the back got up and was motioning for the woman next to him to rise. Slater gestured for the woman to remain seated, though Phoenix saw him look longingly at the bus bench before refusing it. He managed a fractured version of *"Estoy bien,"* but anybody could see he was anything but all right. Meanwhile, he pushed Phoenix down into the seat the Mexican man had vacated. She tried to protest, but it did no good. Thus, she was seated and Slater was standing with a precarious hold on the back of her bench, when the black Ford Bronco bumped the side of the bus full force just beneath the window nearest them. Slater staggered backward and would have fallen if helpful hands hadn't caught him.

Other passengers were being similarly assisted up and down the crowded bus.

"*¿Que pasa?*" someone questioned loudly over the cries and babbling that had broken out.

"It's Sax," Slater said as if in answer.

Slater had righted himself and returned to Phoenix's side where he hovered protectively over her.

"What did you say?" she asked.

"It's the guy from the beach," Slater said. "He's ramming the bus."

Phoenix gasped and turned back toward the window just as the Bronco slammed the side of the bus again. She grabbed on to Slater, and he wrapped his arms around her to keep them both from being knocked to the floor. Phoenix recognized curses and exclamations in Spanish, as some of the passengers waved fists at the windows on the impact side of the bus while others cringed away.

"He's trying to force the bus off the road," Slater said with his arms still tight around her.

Phoenix peered past Slater's sheltering body toward the windows on the other side of the bus. There was a cliff in that direction and sun-sparkled ocean. The bus had careened across the wide, graveled shoulder and almost struck the guardrails.

"We'll go over the cliff," she said. "Everybody on here could be killed."

She pushed out of Slater's arms and up from the seat. She was on her way down the aisle, shoving past agitated passengers, before he could catch up and grab her arm.

"What are you doing?" he asked.

"I can't let the rest of these people get hurt because of us. I'm going to tell the driver to let us off the bus."

She pulled mightily against Slater's grasp. Ordinarily, that would probably have done no good, but his bout with the sea had weakened his grip. She got away and continued down the aisle. That passage was even more treacherous now because the bus had picked up speed. Phoenix stumbled and nearly fell more than once before reaching the driver.

Phoenix was scrambling for the words she needed in Spanish when the driver said, ''*Señorita*, you have to sit down.''

''You speak English?'' she asked, much relieved.

''*Sí*. Now, please sit down.''

She ignored his order. ''You have to let me and my friend off the bus,'' she said. ''The man in the black car is after us.''

The Bronco struck a third time, and shrieks rose from the women passengers as Phoenix pitched forward toward the windshield. She would have crashed into the glass if Slater's sudden grip on her arm hadn't stopped her. She could feel the returned strength in the hold he had on her, perhaps summoned by the prospect of her being injured. Once again, the bus had veered toward the cliff, scraping along the guardrails.

''You have to let us off,'' Phoenix shouted at the driver. ''Then he'll leave you alone.''

The driver had steered the bus back from the rails, but the right side wheels were still on the shoulder of the road. He pressed the accelerator toward the floor, and the bus lurched forward. Phoenix heard gravel hit the side of the bus in a fusillade louder than the cries of the passengers.

''Everybody sit down,'' the driver shouted. ''*¡Sientanse!* Nobody gets off this bus.''

The shouts and curses subsided for a moment.

"I am going to outrun *este diablo,*" the driver said.

"Let us off," Phoenix cried. "We don't want anybody else to get hurt because of us."

"Está bien, señorita," the driver said flashing a smile at her in the rearview mirror. "We have a good chase."

There was a murmur from the seats behind Slater and Phoenix. She turned to see the rest of the passengers grabbing tightly to their seats and to each other. Some had hunkered down in the aisles and were grasping the seat legs that were bolted to the floor. Slater pulled Phoenix to the floor and did the same. The driver laid on the horn. He was steering the bus wildly from one side of the road to the other and hollering phrases in Spanish she couldn't understand. Phoenix strained up out of Slater's arms to see. They were approaching the city limits now. The traffic was heavier here. The driver snaked the bus between and around vehicles, blasting the horn all the while. Phoenix forced herself up far enough to look out the windows on the left side of the bus. There was no black Bronco in sight.

"He's still back there," Slater said. "He's still after us. He won't give up."

"Who is he?" she asked, trying not to sound as panicked as she was beginning to feel.

"Don't you know?"

She glanced back at Slater who was regarding her with a quizzical look on his face.

"Why should I know who he is?" she said. "You're the one he's after."

Slater appeared even more perplexed.

"That's right, isn't it?" she asked. "This is the same man who tried to shoot you at the hotel this morning and then followed us to Pie de la Cuesta?"

Slater studied her face a moment longer. "That's correct," he said at last. "He's after me."

Phoenix felt like asking how Slater could act surprised that she'd figured out what was going on. She'd have to be stupid not to. He didn't think that of her, did he? Of course, this wasn't the place for such inquiries. Slater was holding on to her with one hand. With the other he gripped a seat leg so tightly the cords stood out on his arm. She knew that had to be hurting him, but she didn't tell him to let go. She had no desire to hurtle toward the windshield again. She'd clamped on to Slater just as tight as the driver maneuvered the careening bus at unbelievably high speed through the traffic into Acapulco.

"This guy can really drive," Slater said admiringly.

"*Gracias, señor,*" said the driver.

"The thanks go to you, *amigo,*" Slater responded.

"Now we have to get you two off here safely," the driver said. "Pablo," he called out. "Come here."

A young man dressed in a bellman's uniform, probably on his way to work in one of the city's hotels, leaned forward from the seat behind the driver and next to his ear. They spoke in Spanish for a moment but too fast for Phoenix to make out the words. Pablo sat back, almost toppling onto his seatmate as the bus veered sharply once more. He spoke just as rapidly then to that seatmate who leaned back and passed on the message to the person behind him. Whatever they were saying was quickly communicated among the passengers toward the back and along the sides of the bus.

"What's going on?" Slater asked.

"I don't know," Phoenix said. "I can't understand what they're saying."

"We're making a plan," the driver said.

"What plan?" Phoenix asked.

"You will see."

Phoenix knew she mustn't ask more now. He had to concentrate on driving. They were barreling toward the heart of Acapulco at what had to be approaching rush hour. She bit her lip as the bus swerved perilously close to a Volkswagen taxicab. They were nearing the busy corner across from the street market Phoenix had visited this morning. Just as she was recognizing the landmark the bus slowed, pitching suddenly to the right and up over the curb. The driver yanked back on the handle to slam the door open as the bus pulled to a stop.

"*Andale,*" he shouted as passengers began to pile forward. "You two stay here till I tell you to leave," he said, grabbing Phoenix's arm to keep her from getting off the bus with the rest.

Slater and Phoenix pressed back into the space between the front seat and the driver to let the other passengers get by. "I think we're being rescued," Slater said, shielding Phoenix from the scrambling crowd.

"*Ahora,*" the driver said, pulling at Phoenix's arm. "You two go now."

About half of the passengers were already out of the bus. Slater pushed her to her feet but didn't let go of her.

As they passed the driver, he said, "*Muchas gracias,*" and sounded like he really meant it.

"*De nada, amigo*" was the answer. "*Me gusto mucho.*"

Slater looked questioningly at Phoenix.

"He says he enjoyed it," she translated, wishing she felt the same.

Then Phoenix and Slater were outside the bus in the midst of a crowd with Pablo at their side.

"Keep your heads down," he said, dragging on Slater's arm to bring him down shorter than the surrounding camouflage of bodies.

Slater cooperated, but Phoenix heard him groan at the effort. She also heard Pablo speak to Slater once more.

"This is where I work," he said, pushing something into Slater's palm. "Come there later if you need a place to hide. You will do that best among other *americanos*."

Slater nodded but didn't have time to answer. The crowd was already hustling Slater and Phoenix toward the opposite curb. A pathway opened in front of them then straight to the open door of a waiting cab. They crouched low through the barrage of pats on the back and wishes for *"Buena suerte,"* until they were inside the Beetle and speeding off down the Costera Miguel Aleman into the center of Acapulco. Phoenix raised her head just high enough to peek out the rear window and scan the road behind them. There was no black Bronco in sight. She breathed a sigh of relief, however momentary, and resettled herself in Slater's arms.

Chapter Sixteen

"Vamos a Walmart," Phoenix said to the driver.

"What are you doing?" Slater asked hoping she actually had a plan in mind. He'd had no time to think anything up yet himself.

"We're going to do some more shopping," she said.

"Shopping?"

First the street market this morning, now, if he'd understood right, she was taking them to a Walmart store. He was beginning to think that whenever things got tense she went on a buying spree.

"I'm going to practice my profession just one more time," she said.

"And was exactly does that mean?"

"I'm going to change your image."

"What are you talking about?" Slater asked, though he was beginning to catch a glimmer of what she must be getting at.

"Somebody's after you. Right?"

Slater hesitated. This was the same thing she'd been suggesting back on the bus.

"What makes you think he's after me?" he asked carefully. "Maybe he's after you."

She'd been huddled close to him, exactly where he

wanted her to be. She sat up now and turned toward him.

"You don't have to tell me what you've done," she whispered so the driver wouldn't hear. "I only care about keeping this man, whoever he is, from finding you before we can figure out what to do."

She was staring at him hard and directly into his eyes. He couldn't find a single hint of insincerity in her face. His instincts, and a long history of listening to falsehoods, told him nobody was a good enough liar to look as innocent as she did right now and not be. Slater took a deep breath and decided to go with his instincts, though the suspicion still rankled that even those instincts were being influenced by how beautiful she looked and how soft she felt.

"Okay," he said despite his suspicions. "I'm putty in your hands, but I think you'd better make yourself unrecognizable too."

She looked as if she might disagree.

"Sax has seen you," Slater told her. "He'll be looking for both of us."

Again, as on the bus, she betrayed no sign of being familiar with SideMan's name. Slater had a lot of questions he wanted to ask her about that and other things, but for now he would play along.

"You're right," she agreed nodding. "I don't want this man to find you because of me."

"Exactly."

"What did the man from the bus give you?" she asked, pointing toward his clenched fist.

Slater had all but forgotten about the card Pablo had shoved into his hand. He opened his fingers and looked at the card now.

"It's from the Princess Hotel," Phoenix said, leaning

over to look. "That's where we went to see Porfiro the other morning. The young man from the bus must work there."

"Pablo," Slater said. "His name was Pablo."

"Right. Pablo," she repeated sounding preoccupied. She'd taken the card from Slater's hand and appeared to be reading it over carefully. "Pablo might have a good idea here. What better place to hide than right in plain sight."

Slater didn't know how he felt about going where he might run into Porfiro again. This situation already had enough complications to it. Besides, what would they do for money? His wallet was back at Las Tres Marias, and he'd gotten the impression that Phoenix spent the last of her *pesos* renting those horses on the beach. His answer was soon in coming. The cab pulled into a parking lot in front of a huge building with a tall Walmart sign.

"Go into the underground garage," Phoenix directed the driver.

He nodded. Slater had already taken note that most of the service people in Acapulco spoke English as well as Spanish.

"Wait here. I'm going to the cash machine," Phoenix said, pulling a plastic card from the pocket of her shorts and showing it to the driver. "You wait here, too," she told Slater. "I'll be right back."

"Whatever you say."

At least, now he knew where the money would come from. He suppressed the recurring thought that it might be the loot from Laurent she was tapping into. That didn't matter much to Slater right now. What he had to concentrate on was the fact that they were apparently about to enter a very public place. He'd been keeping an eye out for Sax ever since they got off the bus.

There'd been no sign of either SideMan or the big, black Bronco he was driving. Still, Slater was on the alert. If he had anything to say about it, this would be the shortest shopping spree in Phoenix's history.

Unfortunately, she appeared to be in less of a hurry than he was. Once they were inside the store, she wandered up and down the aisles, studying the shelves and dropping her purchases into the cart she was pushing way too slowly for Slater. Meanwhile, he watched in all directions, wishing he hadn't lost his gun in the ocean. He had a spare hidden back in his room at La Escarpadura, but Sax would be watching that place for sure. Or, he'd have some flunky doing it for him. In Slater's experience, characters like Sax tended to pick up small-time confederates wherever they went, petty criminal types in need of money, to do sneaky little odd jobs. No telling who Sax might have latched on to down here.

Slater watched every face as if it might belong to a potential attacker. He'd like to tell whoever might have gotten mixed up with Sax that he was a real wrong number, the kind of heartless thug who doesn't leave loose ends behind. They'd have to figure that out for themselves. Right now, Slater's job was to keep his eyes peeled for one of those loose ends to show up here. He wasn't quite sure what he'd do if that happened. They were in the hair care products aisle at the moment. Maybe he could dump shampoo on the guy's head and lather him into submission. Slater couldn't help chuckling to himself at how absurdly vulnerable they were. He was very much relieved when they'd finished with Walmart at last. They hailed a cab on the Costera and headed for Pablo's hotel. Slater still had misgivings about going there, but at least they'd have a room with a door they could lock behind them.

The Princess was definitely not Slater's usual digs.
He'd pegged the place for upscale tourist territory the
other day. He generally preferred something a little
closer to the bone, and there was definitely nothing even
near to bare bones here. The lobby was an open-air
atrium with balconies circling it high overhead and supported by tall, mahogany columns. Across the atrium
floor, groupings of plush couches were crowded, mostly
with Americans, who sat along the marble railings surrounding large lobby fountains as well. Beyond these
milling masses, the vast lobby area opened onto grounds
with pools, waterfalls and restaurants in what looked like
every direction. Slater didn't like that. This place was
too big, too open, too busy to keep tabs on efficiently.
He also didn't like the way one guy in a security uniform
was looking at him. Slater knew he was dressed like a
bum right now, but he still didn't want to be treated like
one.

Phoenix took care of at least this concern by sashaying
straight up to the security man and asking for Pablo.
Slater could see the effect her smile had on the hotel
cop. In an instant, he was scrambling off to do her bid-
ding. He probably would have given her his gun if she
asked for it. Slater's cop instincts twitched yet again at
how comfortable Phoenix was with manipulating people,
especially men. He had to conclude she'd had a lot of
practice.

Still, when Pablo came hurrying up to them a few
minutes later and hustled Phoenix and her bank card
cash through the registration process, Slater couldn't
help being grateful for her special talent at greasing
wheels. In no time at all, they were in that locked room
he'd been thinking about. Phoenix was bustling around,
checking out the bathroom, throwing open the doors

onto the terrace, exclaiming about the beach view. Slater was only vaguely aware of all that. He'd plopped down on the bed and was already well on his way to unconsciousness.

SLATER DIDN'T so much wake up as come to. The first thing he heard was the sound of surf hitting a beach. He was reminded of Pie de la Cuesta and SideMan Sax. Slater rolled over, and the cry of his sore muscles was yet another reminder of his last encounter with surf. But where was he now? The room was bright and airy and filled with morning sunshine. Slater pushed himself up onto the mound of pillows someone had propped beneath his head. He remembered now. He was at some big tourist hotel across the bay from the center of Acapulco. He was also nude and alone.

Slater pulled his still aching body out of bed and looked around. On the dresser was a stack of folded clothes. He'd already noticed that the ones he'd had on when he got here were nowhere to be seen. When had they gotten here anyway? It must have been late afternoon, almost evening. It was morning now, the next morning he assumed. He'd slept the evening and night away, maybe sixteen hours or so. He'd never slept that long at one stretch in his life. There was a white, lightweight terry cloth robe at the bottom of the bed. He put it on. Phoenix certainly had them traveling first class. Once again, Slater couldn't help but think of Beldon Laurent's money.

The pile on the dresser didn't do much to quiet his misgivings—very nice threads with tags from shops labeled Princess Hotel Underground Mall. Phoenix had been giving that bank card of hers a workout again this morning. She must have a real cushy nest egg stashed away. She'd bought him shoes, shirts, slacks, underwear, shorts, even a bathing suit all in his size. A note in an envelope bearing the same hotel insignia as that on his bathrobe pocket was propped against the pile of clothes.

"I'll be back soon," it read. "Take a long, soothing shower. Relax. Breakfast is on the terrace." It was signed, "Love, Phoenix," with a drawing of a rising sun after her name.

That signature melted Slater's heart. Whatever suspicions had been gathering there like a dark cloud drifted away into the sunlight. He walked to the terrace doorway. Two cushioned chairs sat next to a low, round table. A tray on the table brimmed over with fresh fruit, pastries, a coffee carafe, china dishes, polished silverware, linen napkins. Slater sat down in one of the chairs and lifted the lid of the carafe. The aroma of Mexican coffee, rich and strong, drew him in. He leaned back against the cushions and gazed out past the terrace wall. The surf he'd heard hitting the beach did so much more calmly here than at Pie de la Cuesta. A fringe of foam washed up on a beautiful, white beach, nothing like the wild, ripping tide of Pie de la Cuesta. As Slater poured his first cup of coffee, he could almost believe he was on a leisurely vacation in paradise—almost, but not quite.

PHOENIX TRIED NOT to let the others in the elevator see how agitated she was, but once she was out of the door onto her floor, she ran all the way to the room. She felt as if she'd been delivered a one-two punch straight to the stomach. Now she had no choice but to do the same to Slater. She burst through the door as he was walking out of the bathroom. He had a white towel wrapped around him, and his hair was wet and wavy. The muscles of his arms and shoulders rippled as he patted his body dry with another towel. For a moment, the gorgeous sight of him made Phoenix forget what she was there to do.

"I still have a hard time lifting my arms very high," he said. "How about helping me dry my hair?"

He handed her the towel and stepped close. She took the towel and reached up to rub his dark waves. That put her flat against his chest. She could feel the moist warmth radiating from his skin and smell the clean scent of him as his arms folded around her.

"You should have been here to take that shower with me," he murmured.

He pulled the tail of the pale peach linen blouse she purchased this morning out of the waistband of her eggshell, loose linen slacks. She'd wanted to think of herself and Slater as just another tourist couple when she picked this outfit from the rack in a dress shop in the underground mall. She'd even coordinated it with beige leather strap sandals and a matching shoulder bag. She could hardly look more normal and benign, but that was only on the surface. She had made these wardrobe selections and put on this outfit before she'd found out the two pieces of shocking news she was here to tell Slater now. She stepped back out of his arms as his lips began a trail of kisses across her eyelids.

"We have to talk," she said.

"We can talk later," he replied, dragging her back into his arms.

She sighed against him. She could feel the pressure of his arousal beneath the bath sheet he had wrapped around him. The taut smoothness of his skin grazed her cheek, and she was nearly lost to the power of her own desire. Somewhere in the depths of her besotted mind, a small but insistent voice told her she could not succumb to temptation now. Phoenix sighed once more and pushed him away again, hard enough this time to get his attention even above the clamoring of his own obvious need for her.

"I mean it, Slater," she said. "We have to talk now. Things have happened that you need to know about. Terrible things."

She turned away from Slater, walked to the bed and sat. The breezy, sunlit terrace beckoned through the open doors, but she couldn't allow herself any more distractions now. She handed Slater the hotel robe that was lying on the bed. He put it on before pulling off the towel he was wearing underneath. Before he could tie his robe, she'd caught a glimpse of dark, tightly curled hair that made her all but moan. It was even more difficult to remind herself to keep on course this time.

"What terrible things are you talking about?" he asked.

Phoenix marveled at how calm he had become, almost as much as she marveled at how that mere glimpse of his body had nearly mesmerized her. She sighed yet again.

"First of all," she said, hearing how dispirited she sounded. "Porfiro is dead."

Slater had stepped back toward the dresser. He leaned there now, against the edge of it, watching her and folding his arms across his chest.

"Does that have something to do with us?" he asked, even more calmly than before.

Phoenix nodded. "He appears to have driven over a cliff on the highway between the city and Pie de la Cuesta."

Slater showed no reaction to that. She went on.

"It happened yesterday afternoon, and it also appears that he was driving your rental Jeep at the time."

Phoenix could feel her pulse pounding and wondered what special talent allowed Slater to remain so steely and in control. A reminder of his probably criminal background flashed through her thoughts, making her feel more dispirited still. Maybe he'd been through lots of situations like this one.

"What makes you think it was my Jeep?" he was asking.

"I put two and two together along with the rest of it."

"What rest of it?"

Phoenix almost sighed again but realized how much she'd been doing that and stopped herself.

"They said he was on a special job for a man with a name like a musical instrument."

Slater was the one to sigh this time. "Sax," he said.

"That was my thought."

"Who were 'they?'"

"What?"

"The people who told you about Sax and Porfiro. Who were they?"

"Pablo was actually the one who told me. He heard about what happened to Porfiro from the other tour drivers at the stand in front of the hotel here. Pablo also put two and two together. The place where the crash happened, you and me making our getaway down the same road, the fact that when the tour drivers saw this man Sax, he was driving a black Ford Bronco."

"Has Pablo told anybody else about this?"

"I don't think so."

"Is he still around the hotel?"

"He was in the lobby just now before I came up here."

Slater stared off toward the open terrace doors. Phoenix guessed he wasn't seeing the sunlight or hearing the sounds of the surf and laughter from the beach and pool-side several stories below.

"Maybe we should find Pablo and make it worth his while not to share his conclusions with anyone else," Slater said.

"If you're talking about paying him to keep his mouth shut, I already tried that and he refused. I don't think he'll tell anybody about us."

"What makes you think that?"

Slater's cool way of questioning her felt like an interrogation. Phoenix didn't like that feeling.

"Because he seemed sympathetic to me," she replied, knowing how flimsy that sounded. "And he said that Porfiro was mixed up in a lot of shady deals. Pablo didn't approve of that."

"Did Pablo actually say that or do you just think he sounded like he might feel that way?"

"He actually said it."

Her annoyance at this third degree was beginning to show, but Slater didn't appear to notice.

"How do you know it was my rental that Porfiro was driving for sure?" Slater asked, grilling her still.

"I don't know for sure, but it was a silver Jeep from one of the agencies at the airport. It was also headed back from Pie de la Cuesta at about the same time your Jeep went missing. That sounds like two and two to me."

"Two and two," Slater said, nodding slowly. He was silent for a moment before continuing. "What else?"

"What do you mean, 'what else?'" Phoenix wasn't

following his train of thought fast enough to keep up. That made her more exasperated still.

"You said terrible *things* happened. That's plural. Did all of those terrible things have to do with Porfiro, or is there something else?"

"Yes, there is something else."

Phoenix had the urge to jump up from the bed and slap the cool, distant expression off Slater's face. She couldn't believe he was treating her this way. She gripped the bedclothes on either side of where she was sitting to keep herself from acting on that urge.

"In case you really give a damn, and I doubt that you do," she went on as one hot tear slid down her cheek, "my grandfather's friend, Citrone Blue, has been kidnapped and if we don't do something about it he's going to end up as dead as poor Porfiro."

The rest of the tears came then. She squeezed her eyes shut but they wouldn't stop. Suddenly, Slater was next to her on the bed, holding her in his arms and murmuring comforting words into her ear. Fortunately, he didn't ask any more questions for a while.

Chapter Seventeen

Slater held Phoenix and rocked her gently while her sobs quieted to whimpers. She'd been through so much these past few days. She had to be close to bursting from it all and maybe from the secrets she couldn't tell as well. Everything he'd found out about her in their brief but intense acquaintance indicated that she was not the deceitful type by nature. Secrets, especially dark secrets, can build up tremendous pressure inside an honest person. This is one of the things a cop learns. That particular lesson came in very handy in an interrogation room. Manipulating the suspect's guilt about lying is a prime technique for extracting confessions. Right now, however, Slater wished he hadn't studied that lesson quite so effectively. Right now, he was feeling some guilt for a deceit of his own. Phoenix trembled in his arms, and he almost blurted out the whole truth to her on the spot. Luckily or not, his cop mentality remained strong. The moment passed, and he said nothing as Phoenix gradually calmed herself to stillness again.

"I care," Slater said softly.

"What did you say?"

"A few minutes ago you said I probably don't care that your friend is in trouble. I'm just telling you that's not true. I care about anything that makes you unhappy.''

Phoenix turned in his arms and looked up at him. Women were supposed to look a mess when they cried. She just looked flushed and moist with her eyes shining. Slater's heart thumped so hard he couldn't breathe for a minute, maybe two.

''I thought you didn't like Mr. Blue,'' she said.

''It isn't that I don't like him so much as that I don't trust him.''

''Why don't you trust him? You hardly know him.''

Slater almost blew it and told her how his cop sense gave him clues about people the instant he met them.

''I just have a feeling about him,'' Slater said instead.

Phoenix stood up fast from the bed and brushed off her slacks. That was the first time Slater had noticed she was wearing a new outfit. She looked very sophisticated and chic, even more of a woman than she was in her short shorts. Unfortunately, she didn't give him much time to admire this new facet of her beauty. She had grabbed her purse from the bed and was headed for the door.

Slater jumped up and followed.

''Where are you going?'' he said, waylaying her as she reached for the doorknob.

''You have a feeling,'' she said with more than a little anger in her voice. ''Well, I have a feeling, too. My feeling is that my grandfather's oldest, dearest friend is in trouble and I'm going to help him.''

''Wait a minute.''

Slater put his hands on her shoulders. His heart hurt as he registered the tension there from her holding herself rigid in resistance of him.

''What do you want?'' she snapped. ''I've already

wasted precious time sitting up here bawling like a baby. The message said they'd do something to him if I didn't come soon.''

''What message?''

How could anyone have gotten a message to her? Nobody knew where they were. At least, that's what Slater hoped, especially since he had a terrible suspicion that the ''they'' she was referring to was Sax and his hired thugs.

''I called La Escarpadura and checked my room voice mail. There was a message from Citrone. He sounded terrified. You have to let me go to him.''

''I'm coming with you.''

''No, you are not.''

Phoenix pushed at Slater. The move took him by surprise, and he stumbled backward as she reached past him to the door and pulled it open.

''Wait,'' he commanded, knowing how futile that sounded in the face of her obvious determination. ''I'm with you for this ride whether you want me there or not.''

''I'm not waiting for anything. If you insist on tagging along where you're not wanted, then you'd better get a move on.''

She was out the door then and walking in long, purposeful strides down the hall. Slater grabbed garments from the dresser and pulled them on fast—briefs, slacks, a polo shirt, deck shoes. He was still pulling off store tags as he dashed out into the hall and yanked the door shut behind him. With some luck, the elevator would be slow arriving and he'd catch up with Phoenix before she got on. It occurred to Slater that, with him in these duds and her in those slacks and that blouse, anybody who saw them would be bound to think, ''Look at that nice, normal couple.'' How wrong they would be. On the other hand, Phoenix's efforts at changing their image were already taking effect.

PHOENIX HAD RENTED another Jeep for the day before she called Escarpadura and heard that frightening voice mail message. Citrone's distress had been unmistakable. He said she had to come to the place she'd scrawled on a piece of paper from her purse or the people who had abducted him promised to hurt him badly, maybe even kill him. The time signature on the message tape indicated that he'd called three hours ago, which meant he could be in even worse trouble by now. That realization sent Phoenix scurrying out of the elevator the instant the doors slid open at lobby level.

Another elevator had arrived at the same time, and Slater stepped out of it to follow hot on her heels. She thought about telling him one more time to stay here at the hotel, but she doubted that would do much good. The best she could do was to make certain he didn't feel particularly welcome. With that in mind, she didn't say a word to him or even glance in his direction as they walked fast across the elegant hotel lobby, rounding the fountain on their way to the front entrance and the parking lot where the rentals were kept.

"Let me drive," Slater said as they approached the lot attendant's booth and Phoenix pulled the Jeep rental agreement from her purse.

"The vehicle is in my name," she said. "I have to drive."

She wished that weren't the case. She really didn't feel like taking on the responsibility of being behind the wheel at the moment.

"I can take over as soon as we get out of this guy's

range,'' Slater said quietly as they came into earshot of the attendant.

Phoenix nodded. That sounded like a good plan to her. The attendant took the agreement and pointed out a Jeep. Remembering that other Jeep also reminded her of what had happened to it. She grabbed the agreement papers back just a bit too abruptly, and the attendant looked at her curiously.

"Muchas gracias," she said quickly and pushed a tip into his hand.

That brought a broad smile to his lips. *"Muchas gracias* to you, *señorita,"* she heard him calling after her as she took off toward the Jeep with Slater, once again, right behind her.

Phoenix let Slater take over the driving not far from the hotel entrance. He sped away almost before she could get her seat belt on. She'd already told him the instructions Citrone had left on her voice mail. They were to go to the village of Coyuca and wait at the *cantina* just off the main street at the side of the river. Phoenix had never been to Coyuca. She did know it was on the same highway as Pie de la Cuesta but much farther along. Part of renting a vehicle in Acapulco was the signing of an agreement not to drive that far beyond the city. The first time she rented a car she'd read that document thoroughly. It left her wondering just exactly what the rental company might be worried about. Tourist encounters with *bandidos?* With *federales?* Both? There was no spare tire in any of the rentals she'd seen here. She suspected that was an additional incentive to keep *turistas* close to town. Phoenix didn't give a damn, at the moment, about violating her rental agreement, or about *bandidos* or *federales,* either. But, she did hope they wouldn't get a flat tire.

Meanwhile, she was aware that she hadn't been behaving as rationally as usual, at least not since she slammed down the phone after hearing Citrone Blue's message. Who was he, anyway? Somebody her grandfather had shared some good times with decades ago. Somebody she knew as little about as she'd accused Slater of knowing. Yet, she'd never really questioned that she would do everything in her power to help him, including this drive at top speed down the highway into whatever might lie ahead.

If asked for a reason for her behavior, as she had a feeling she would be asked by Slater eventually, she'd have to say there probably was no reason in terms of the precise definition of that word. What she was doing now had nothing to do with reason. She was acting on pure emotion. Her grandfather had meant everything to her, and he would want her to save his friend. Whether that expectation was reasonable or rational didn't matter to Phoenix at the moment.

"Did Blue mention who snatched him?" Slater asked shortly after he took over the driving.

"Who else?" Phoenix said, marveling at how cold and flat her voice sounded all of a sudden. "The same person who's been doing everything he can to screw up our lives for the past three days. I guess he's using Citrone now to get to you through me. He must have seen me with Citrone or found out from the hotel clerk or God knows what."

Slater glanced over at her. "Are you talking about Sax?"

"Yes, of course. Sax. As I said, who else?"

That was when Slater's foot had tromped down to the floor and they'd started moving at top speed.

They weren't very far past the turnoff to Pie de la

Cuesta when the scenery began to change. Phoenix imagined this was what people were talking about when they referred to "the real Mexico." The land had a rough look to it with clumps of vegetation and trees between the modest homesteads of a small house and several outbuildings set in a patch of mostly dirt. Pigs, goats and cackling chickens roamed free through these farmyards. Phoenix and Slater passed a field of Brahman cattle as rawboned and strange as this region. But that was only off to the right side of the road. To the left, the landscape was much more lush and green, almost as if they were driving down the dividing line between two Mexicos, one hardscrabble dirt farm country and the other a tropical paradise. Phoenix had experienced both in the past few days.

Meanwhile, she and Slater were the objects of some interest to the occasional farm folk along Highway 200. Apparently, they encountered few *gringos* out here. The longer they drove, the more ill at ease Phoenix became with how far out of their element they were venturing. The town of Coyuca, when they finally reached it, made her most aware of that. The main street was lined with rundown stores and *cantinas,* poorer than the poorest buildings she'd seen in Acapulco. Her gaze was met with cool stares from the local citizens clustered in front of the buildings, letting her know how much she did not belong. It occurred to her that if she and Slater got into trouble here, they might not find the locals as helpful as they'd been on that white-and-blue bus yesterday.

She was relieved when they left the crowded main street and turned into a quieter road along the river. Slater pulled up in front of an open-air *cantina* with multicolored Christmas lights strung along the edge of the roof. Mexican music played on a radio. Unfortunately, the twinkling lights and lilting music did little to put Phoenix in a less apprehensive mood. She followed Slater to a table on the river side of the *cantina*. The waitress took their order for two colas then shuffled away. Phoenix tried to watch the women beating their laundry against white rocks beneath the nearby bridge over the river. Ordinarily, she would have found that fascinating. Today she was too agitated to concentrate on the rustic scene.

She could tell that Slater was agitated, too. His occasional glances around the *cantina* and along the road outside and the riverbank might appear casual to anyone who didn't know him, but Phoenix sensed intense alertness in the surveillance he was keeping. Still, there was no sign of Sax or anybody who might have been working for him, either. Nobody was paying much attention to Phoenix and Slater at all. Then, the waitress returned with two sweating bottles of soft drinks on a small, round tray. A folded piece of paper lay between the bottles.

"Señor McCain?" she said to Slater.

"*Sí,*" he said. "I'm Señor McCain."

"This is for you."

She indicated the folded paper on the tray. Phoenix was impressed by the way Slater managed to maintain his cool facade even then. He picked up the paper as if he couldn't have cared less what message it contained. He rummaged in his pocket for *pesos* for the waitress and smiled as he put them in her hand. She smiled back, and the flash of her dark eyes reminded Phoenix of how attractive Slater really was. She put her hand on top of his on the table in a gesture she was surprised to make. The waitress shrugged her shoulders and walked away, swinging her hips rather than shuffling this time. Slater's hand was warm beneath Phoenix's palm. She could feel both strength and tension there.

"It's from Sax," he said and pulled his hand away from hers. "Let's go."

They left the bottles of cola untouched on the table and hurried to the Jeep. Slater was already behind the wheel with the engine revving as Phoenix ran around to her side and hopped in.

"Where are we going?" she shouted over the engine roar as Slater's foot hit the gas pedal and they jolted out onto the road.

He tossed the note into her lap as response. Phoenix read the brief message. It told them to continue along this road from the *cantina* for approximately five miles until they came to a brickworks on the right side of the road. It didn't say what would happen then.

Chapter Eighteen

Slater didn't like the feel of any of this. He had no idea where he was headed. All he was sure of was that there'd be trouble waiting. He wouldn't have minded that so much. He might not even have minded being on a road the map didn't mention, but Phoenix was with him. That made all the difference.

Slater had a cop's natural love for the special kick a little danger carries with it. As long as he kept the odds pretty much on his side, he welcomed the occasional adventure just to keep his blood moving and his edges sharp. He didn't welcome anything about this morning. He didn't give a damn about Citrone Blue or want to be tearing around the countryside after him. In fact, he was tempted to fake a vehicle breakdown and abort this trip altogether. Too bad he couldn't do that and his job, too.

Slater had belongings strewn across the landscape in three hotel rooms—at the Princess, Las Tres Marias and La Escarpadura—none of which they'd ever officially checked out of. He was accustomed to picking up and moving on at the spur of the moment when an assignment called for a quick change of venue, but this was ridiculous. Phoenix, on the other hand, appeared to take it all in her stride. Even now, she just sat there next to him without comments as the Jeep bounced over the rutted road to God knows where. Slater wondered what kind of history could have made her so cool while he was spiking toward the opposite end of the temperature scale. He'd once had a reputation for being quick-tempered, but over the years he'd learned to keep himself under control. These days, he thought of his hot-headedness as a secret weapon he could whip out of his kit bag of tricks when he needed extra firepower. This morning, however, he was feeling less and less in that kind of control. Part of that agitation came from not having a gun.

The situation ahead was going to involve a confrontation. He'd bet his badge on that, and no smart cop goes into a fight unarmed if he can help it. As if to second that thought, Slater's right eyelid twitched tightly, the way it had a habit of doing when he was about to make a big mistake. Sometimes he heeded that warning. Sometimes he didn't pay much attention to it at all. This morning, he knew he had to do the former. One gun was in a faraway hotel room. The other was currently being buffeted by surf and tide at Pie de la Cuesta and probably had buried itself deep under shifting sand by now.

They should have stopped at La Escarpadura to pick up his spare sidearm on the way out of the city, but he'd had a strong feeling Phoenix would take off without him the minute he was out of the car. Nothing could bring Slater's anger to fever pitch faster than feeling frustrated, like he did right now. He had to do something, whether it improved their circumstances or not. The alternative— letting events roll over him like one of those waves at Pie de la Cuesta—was unthinkable for him.

Slater whipped the steering wheel to the right and skidded the Jeep onto the shoulder of the road.

"What are you doing?" Phoenix cried out.

She gripped the window frame on her side to keep from being bumped out of her seat as Slater wheeled into a U-turn.

"We're going back to town," he said.

"What town?"

"The last one." The name of the place had escaped him for the moment.

"Coyuca?"

"Right. Coyuca."

"What are we going there for?"

Slater didn't answer. He didn't know how to tell her in a way she'd be able to accept that he was about to troll the streets of an unfamiliar village in a foreign country for somebody who could sell him serious firepower. What he had to ask her, whether or not he knew how, was for the means to make that transaction happen.

"I need to ask you a favor," he shouted as the Jeep rattled and banged in and out of the frequent ruts he was hitting entirely too fast.

"How big a favor?"

Slater glanced over at her. That wasn't what he'd expected her to ask.

"I want you to give me every penny you have with you."

"Is that why you're heading in the opposite direction from where we're supposed to be going? Because you need money?"

"You're not the only one who likes to shop."

She didn't smile, but another glance told him her expression had softened. She reached into the beige leather purse she'd been carrying by a long, narrow strap over her shoulder ever since they left the Princess. She pulled out a bundle of cash.

"This is all I have," she said. "I have credit cards, too, and a bank card."

"I don't think there'll be a cash machine where we're going."

They'd reached the turn from the riverbank road onto Coyuca's main street. Shabby buildings and not too well heeled people confirmed Slater's guess about the bank card machine. Slater pulled the Jeep to the side of the narrow, dusty street and yanked the emergency brake handle to make sure they didn't slide down the slight grade. He hesitated to take the folded bills from her hand, but he had no choice.

"Thanks," he said and pocketed the money. "Wait here. I'll be right back."

Their arrival in the center of Coyuca had not gone unnoticed. A number of nearby citizens had been watching the Jeep closely ever since it pulled to a stop. Slater imagined they had also observed the cash changing hands between himself and Phoenix. That might explain why a perfect stranger wearing a too-wide smile was walking toward Slater now.

"*¿Qué pasa, señor?*" the stranger said. "*Me llamo Miguel.*"

Slater figured out that the guy was introducing himself. Slater pointed at his own chest and said, "McCain. *Señor* McCain."

Beyond that, Slater had no idea how he was going to communicate well enough with anybody to complete his transaction. His Spanish was really bad.

"*Tenemos dinero para una pistola.*"

The voice came from behind Slater. He whirled around to find Phoenix smiling at Miguel. She spoke quietly to him for a while longer until he hurried away.

"What did you say to him?" Slater asked. He had a

suspicion what the answer might be, but he found it too good to believe.

"I told him we wanted to buy a gun."

Phoenix stared up at Slater with a subdued expression, and then she walked into his arms. Right there, in the middle of that village street with dozens of curious men, women and children looking on, Slater buried his face in the sweetness of her hair and wished he could save her from whatever lay ahead. That he would whisk her away from here to one of those wide, white beaches she liked so much. They would bask in the sun and make love at *siesta* time. He would protect her from all things dangerous, or even upsetting, forever.

Then, Miguel returned with a crumpled paper bag under his arm, and Slater's fantasy of peace and protection evaporated on a breath of tropical breeze.

PHOENIX HAD MADE SURE Miguel understood that she wanted a powerful weapon. She knew enough about guns to recognize that a revolver wouldn't do. Ordinarily, she hated guns, but she'd left ordinary considerations behind long ago. She'd decided to take up with a man who had to be a criminal, and she had helped him arm himself, with no less than a semiautomatic weapon. She should have been surprised that such a pistol was so readily available on the streets of a small Mexican village, but she was from New York City. She knew that just about anything could be made available to anybody who had the price. She'd apparently had the price in Coyuca. Now, she and Slater were on their way to a showdown. Citrone Blue was only an excuse for this test of who would win and who would lose, the bad guys or the not-quite-as-bad guys, Slater being the latter. Phoenix could hardly believe how calm she felt, like the stillness before a storm.

She smelled the brickworks before she saw it. The acrid smoke of kiln fires drifted along the road and hazed the sky. Piles of bricks came into view as the Jeep jounced around a curve in the makeshift road which had grown less and less drivable the farther they traveled from Coyuca. Beyond the neat stacks of adobes in orange earth colors row on row near the roadside, were two outbuildings. The larger one, set at a distance from the road, had to be the kiln shed. Smoke from the brick chimney made that obvious. The second building, small and off to the side, must have been the office headquarters for this little operation. The ground was flat and dusty but well ordered, as if somebody must sweep it regularly. Wheelbarrows lined the wall of the kiln shed, and a hill of sandbags had been heaped up nearby. Someone took good care of this work site. Still, something was very wrong. It was the middle of the workday, not yet *siesta* hour, but the place was deserted.

"Where is everybody?" she asked as they crept out of the Jeep. "Shouldn't there be a work crew here?"

"I was thinking the same thing."

Slater signaled for her to duck down behind the Jeep. He had his weapon drawn and was crouched at the alert as Phoenix sidestepped to stand next to him.

"What are we going to do now?" she asked.

"*We* aren't doing anything. You stay here out of range behind this Jeep and keep your head down. I'm going in there." He gestured toward the headquarters building that really wasn't much more than a hut. "If I don't come out in five minutes, take the Jeep and go for the police. You can ask in Coyuca where the nearest police station is."

"That's not the way it's going to be," Phoenix said.

Slater turned toward her with what she was sure must be his most commanding gaze.

"Please, don't give me a hard time," he said. "These people mean business."

"I have no doubt that they do, which is why I'm going in there by myself."

"Are you crazy? You're not doing any such thing."

Phoenix gripped Slater's arm and favored him with her own commanding gaze.

"My instructions were to come out here on my own," she said. "Whoever is inside this place may have seen me drive up with you. That could mean Citrone is in more trouble than ever now. I don't want to be the cause of him getting hurt any more than they may have hurt him already. That's why I'm going in first, and you can back me up."

"You *are* crazy. You could be the one who gets hurt."

"They kidnapped Citrone and made him lure me out here. I don't think they'll hurt me until they have whatever they may be after."

Slater studied her with an unreadable expression on his face. She wondered if he was thinking the same thing that had occurred to her, that he was in fact what they wanted from her, that they'd only brought her out here because they figured Slater would follow.

"We'll go in together, and that's that," he said at last.

Phoenix could tell she wasn't going to be able to talk him out of this decision. She shrugged, then nodded and began to move around the Jeep along the side farthest away from the building.

"Keep your head down," he said sharply.

"Of course, I'll keep my head down. Do you think I'm stupid?"

Still, she took his advice and crouched closer to the ground. At every second, she expected bullets to whiz over her head, but none came. She could imagine Sax and his henchmen inside, biding their time, maybe until they saw the whites of her eyes. She swallowed over the lump of fear in her throat and continued around the Jeep.

"We'll make a dash for the building over there," Slater whispered just behind her.

He motioned toward the side of the building across the dusty, rutted driveway from the Jeep. Phoenix took a deep breath. They'd be in the open there. She peeked up over the Jeep hood far enough to see the window in the shanty wall. Nobody was visible there. They must have ducked down out of sight when they heard the Jeep pull in.

"I'll go first," Slater said.

He moved to push past her, but Phoenix darted out from behind the Jeep as fast as she could go with her body crouched low to make herself as small a target as possible. She couldn't help wondering if she'd feel the bullet hit her before or after she heard it fired. She struck the building wall much harder than she'd meant to and breathing as raggedly as if she'd run the length of the yard instead of only the few feet from the Jeep. Slater was next to her in an instant.

"Sorry about slamming into the wall," she said. "If they didn't know we were here before, they know now."

"Never mind about that. Are you all right?"

Phoenix nodded. "I'm fine."

"I told you to let me go first."

Phoenix put her finger to her lips to shut him up.

She'd already begun creeping along the side of the building.

"I said, me first," Slater repeated as vehemently as was possible in a whisper.

He surged past her, rolling along her body as he pressed close to avoid leaving the shelter of the building's overhanging eaves. Phoenix felt an electric connection through her thin, tropical clothing.

"Keep an eye on the brick pile," he said, pointing toward the stack of adobes near the road.

He was right. Somebody could be lurking there. She watched the brick pile and tried to listen for sounds of movement over the pounding of her heart. They crouched lower still under the window to be as far as possible from the eye line of the sill. Phoenix's expensive linen slacks dragged in the dirt, but she didn't care. She'd let go of the hope of looking her best during this vacation way back when they were being shot at in the parking lot of La Escarpadura.

Slater was at the corner of the building and around it at the same moment. A sudden flash of terror for him made her reach out to hold him back, but her hand clutched empty air as the words, *Don't go,* formed on her lips. She kept silent andhurried around the corner after Slater, hoping that if she moved fast enough she might outdistance this new fear. She glanced over her shoulder in the direction of the brick pile, fully expecting a crowd of *bandidos,* wearing belts of spare bullets across their chests, to come charging at her with guns blazing. Nothing like that happened, but she could taste the terror in her throat as if it had.

Meanwhile, Slater was at one side of the doorway to the shack. He gestured for her to take the other side, and she obeyed by flattening herself against the wall. She

was amazed that her body could move so rapidly when
what she really wanted to do was freeze into a petrified
state. Slater clamped the butt of his gun in both hands
as he surveyed the yard, following the path of his glance
with the aimed barrel of the gun. Phoenix saw him tense,
the muscles of his neck taut above the open collar of his
polo shirt, the large knots of his biceps gone suddenly
hard and flexing beneath the rolled-up edges of his shirt
sleeves.

Before she had time to conclude that he was preparing
to spring into action, he leapt in front of the closed door
and his foot shot out with the sole flat to strike the door
surface hard. The weathered planking splintered beneath
his powerful onslaught, and one more kick sent it crash-
ing open. Slater leapt back against the wall with his gun
pointed toward the doorway. Breathless instants passed,
but Phoenix heard nothing at first from beyond the shattered door. She wondered if that might be because her
breathing was so loud there would be no chance of hearing anything else. Then, the sound of a moan sifted
through her fear, and she remembered all of a sudden
why she was here.

"Citrone," she breathed and lunged for the doorway.

Slater was after her in a shot, but not in time. She was
through the doorway and into the room before she could
think what peril she might be putting herself in. Luckily,
nobody charged out of a corner to attack her, no gunfire
rang out. In fact, the only person in the simple, sparsely
furnished room was Citrone, crumpled and bloody on
the floor. Phoenix darted to his side.

"What have they done to you?" she cried.

Citrone didn't answer. His eyes had gone very wide.

He lifted a trembling finger to point beyond Phoenix's shoulder at the spot where Slater was now standing.

"Don't let him near me," Citrone gasped. "He's one of them."

Chapter Nineteen

What Slater had decided now went into happening. Phoenix was about to find out the truth—at least one layer of what was supposed to be the truth, the next deceptive layer of all.

"He's one of them," Citrone blurted again, his face contorting with the effort.

Even now, Slater bent down to straddle the skin of the phone line.

"...to stay away from me," the old man gasped.

"Don't let him touch me," the gazer frantically past Slater at Phoenix. "I told you, he's one of them."

Phoenix tight... voice... place the big little blue said, man stood back as if this one would—down at him.

"You must be mistaken," Jane said low. "Phoenix my friend Mr. Mix sir. You met him at my hotel the other day. Then's when you met the intruder of..."

Slater could hear the plea in her voice. He could see in her face how desperately she wanted what she was saying to be true; she could find so much there and what looked free information, as if there expecting something like the truth anew.

"No, no," Citrone whispered from the floor. "They told me about him. They told me how they armed him."

Chapter Nineteen

What Slater had dreaded most was now happening. Phoenix was about to find out the truth—or at least one layer of what was supposed to be the truth, the most damning layer of all.

"He's one of them," Citrone Blue said again, his face contorting with the effort.

He'd been shot. Slater knelt down to examine the extent of the wounds.

"You stay away from me," the old man gasped. "Don't let him touch me." He gazed frantically past Slater at Phoenix. "I told you, he's one of them."

Phoenix hadn't moved since the first time Blue said that. She'd knelt at his side, staring down at him.

"You must be mistaken," she said now. "This is my friend Mr. McCain. You met him at my hotel the other day. That's what you must be thinking of."

Slater could hear the plea in her voice. He could see in her eyes how desperately she wanted what she was saying to be true. He could also see doubt there and what looked like resignation, as if she'd been expecting something like this all along.

"No, no," Blue spluttered from the floor. "They told me about him. They told me how they hired him."

Slater backed off a little, though he wished he could shut the old man up right there. Slater would take Phoenix somewhere quiet then. He'd tell her everything, and together they'd figure out a way to extricate her from the trouble she was in. But, he couldn't do that. A man was bleeding on the floor. Slater McCain, the lawman, had to take care of Citrone Blue, the victim.

"Who hired Slater?" Phoenix was asking.

"A man named Sax and the one he works for from New York City," Blue said. "They were both here just before you came."

Slater froze in the act of kneeling beside Blue again. So, Laurent was in town. That struck Slater as very bad news. Laurent would have come here because he wanted the job he'd hired Slater for done and over with. Laurent would be determined to get his money back, and after that he'd want Phoenix dead. Slater was probably also included in that hit contract package by now. Sax would have told Laurent how Slater switched sides and was trying to save Phoenix. Despite all of that, a man was bleeding on the floor. Whatever Slater's misgivings might be about Citrone Blue, he had to be the priority of the moment.

"We can straighten all of that out later," Slater said, pressing forward again and onto one knee next to Blue. "Let me get a look at how badly hurt you are."

"I said, don't touch me."

Blue cringed away. He even tried to raise himself from the floor.

"Slater, what is he talking about?" Phoenix asked.

She still knelt on the opposite side of where Blue lay. A bloodstain was seeping along one leg of her light-colored slacks. Slater could feel that stain creeping over him too, maybe never to be completely washed out again. Undercover work was like that sometimes. The good guys got permanently tainted by the bad guys' dirt. Slater had never really cared much about that before. He cared now.

"We can talk about all of that later," he said to Phoenix with his heart hurting almost as much as if he'd taken the bullet instead of Blue. "I'll explain, and then you can explain your side, too."

"My side?" She sounded truly confused. "I don't have a side. What are you talking about?"

"He thinks you stole a lot of money from this New York City man, the one with the small eyes and the diamond ring on his finger," Blue said. Oddly enough, he appeared to be stronger now rather than weaker. "That's the man who said you worked for him before you came here to Mexico."

"Beldon Laurent?" Phoenix stared from Blue to Slater and back again. "Beldon Laurent is here in Acapulco?"

Slater watched her carefully. He would have expected her to be fearful at finding out the man she stole from was hot on her trail. Instead, all that Slater saw in her face as she'd turned back to him was bewilderment.

"What is going on here?" she asked. "You know, don't you?"

He couldn't help but sigh. He felt the same heavy sinking in his belly as when, in his experience on the force, he'd had to tell families they'd lost somebody they love. This time, however, Slater was pretty sure he'd be the one doing the mourning. Before he could think what to say in response to Phoenix's plea for understanding, Blue gave the answer. He even managed to prop himself up on one elbow to do it. From that, Slater concluded that the wound was probably not life threatening.

"I know the truth," Blue said to Phoenix. "They talked in front of me, Sax and the man you call Laurent. I heard them say that Laurent had hired this man you're with to find you. Laurent told him you'd stolen a lot of money from him. Sax told me that, too, when he first came to my house."

"Money? What money?" Phoenix said. "I didn't steal any money from anybody."

Slater had heard that "I'm innocent, I didn't do it" line a thousand times before. This time it sounded real, but that could be wishful thinking on his part. Still, he held on to the hope that it wasn't.

"That's what the other man, Sax's boss, told him," Blue was saying. "There never was any money stolen. Your boss had to get to you because of something you found out about him. He said you know too much."

"Something I found out about Beldon Laurent? I don't know what you're talking about."

Phoenix sounded more definitely bewildered still. Meanwhile, Slater felt suddenly elated. That might be a strange reaction given the overall circumstances here, but he couldn't help it. She wasn't a thief, after all. The whole thing had been a setup. Laurent told Slater the theft story to convince him to follow Phoenix without letting him know she'd uncovered some kind of dirt on Laurent. He'd have been taking precautions against Slater worming that incriminating information out of her then using it himself against Laurent, probably to extort money out of him. Crooks like Laurent were always worried about things like that. They thought everybody they ran into was made of the same foul stuff they were.

"The one you call Laurent said you were poking around in his past where you had no business to be, and you found out something about him he doesn't want anybody to know," Blue continued.

"I was doing the job he hired me to do," Phoenix said. "Researching his past was part of that job, but I didn't find anything significant enough for him to go to all this trouble over. I realized he wasn't a very nice man and probably had been involved in some shady dealings, but nothing more specific than that. I decided I didn't want to work for him because of what I suspected might be true, but it was a suspicion, nothing more."

Slater's elation mounted higher. She really was innocent. She really hadn't done anything wrong, definitely not anything against the law. He could hear that in her voice and see it in her beautiful eyes. He'd stake his reputation on it.

"You must have found out something bad," Blue said. "Bad enough for Laurent to want to have you killed." He pointed a trembling finger at Slater. "He hired that man you call your friend to do that, to kill you."

Phoenix stared at Slater. Her mouth had fallen open, but she didn't speak. Something had crowded the bewilderment out of her eyes. He saw disbelief there now, and maybe the beginning of fear. He could almost hear the puzzle pieces of her experiences with him starting to click into a recognizable pattern in her head.

"It isn't what you think," Slater said.

He reached toward her, but she shied away. Blue had slipped back down to the floor between them. Slater knew he should be taking care of the bleeding victim. He had to do that now and explain himself to Phoenix later. It was Slater's duty to behave like a cop. God help him, he wished he didn't have to follow that duty call right now, but he was what he was. He couldn't change that.

"How do you know all of this?"

She asked Blue that before Slater could act on his resolve to be a lawman first and a man second. He waited to hear the answer.

"Because they hired me, too."

Blue sounded more exasperated than ashamed. The old guy had been working both sides of the fence and he'd ended up bleeding on the floor of this shack for it.

"Laurent hired you?" Phoenix asked.

Blue shook his head slowly. "No, not him. The other one. The one who works for him. Sax."

"If Sax hired you, you were working for Laurent," Phoenix said. She sounded pretty exasperated herself. "It seems that everybody was working for Laurent."

"But I did not agree to hurt anyone," Blue protested. "I was only supposed to get to know you and see if I could find out anything about where you had the money. That is all he said he wanted from me. Then I came here and found out the true reason he wanted me to bring you to this place."

He was weaker now, his voice less vehement than before. Slater could have stepped in then, but the cop part of him hung back long enough to hear what Blue had to say.

"What true reason was that?" Slater asked because he needed the answer for the report he'd have to be writing on all of this soon.

"You know what I'm talking about already," Blue snapped though his energy was visibly draining by the second.

"*I* don't know what you're talking about," Phoenix said. "Tell me."

"They used me to get you out here to this remote place," Blue said to her. "They paid off the brick makers to leave for the afternoon. Laurent was going to have Sax strangle you to keep you quiet about whatever it is they think you know. Then, I think they were going to put your body in the kiln. Mine, too, I would imagine. When I found out they were planning to murder you, I said I didn't want any part of it and tried to get away. That was when they shot me. They would have shot me again if I didn't lie still and pretend to be dead."

Blue was breathing with more difficulty now. His long confession had obviously used up most of his remaining strength. Nonetheless, Slater had to take the interrogation a couple of steps further.

"Who specifically shot you?" he asked.

"Your friend, Sax," Blue answered feebly.

"Where did they go?" Slater pressed on. "Why did they leave before we got here?"

"There wasn't supposed to be any shooting." Blue was managing only a whisper now. "Laurent said that to Sax. Laurent had wanted to keep everything quiet. He said they would get you later." Blue was looking at Phoenix when he said that. He managed to lift his head a few inches off the floor once more. "That is why you must get away from this man." Blue nodded toward Slater. "He is not your friend. He is one of them."

Blue sank back into what looked like a faint, breathing raggedly. Slater reached to feel for Blue's pulse, but Phoenix grabbed Slater's arm.

"Keep your hands off him," she commanded.

Her eyes had gone steely cold. He saw her gaze slide to the gun still in his hand.

"What he's telling you isn't true," Slater said, aware

that he sounded almost as feeble as Blue had a moment ago.

"It looked to me like he was telling the truth."

The chill in her voice cut Slater to the bone. He felt a sudden stab of sorrow, too, as if something precious had just evaporated in his hand and was gone forever.

"He's only telling you what he thinks to be true," Slater said. He almost wished he didn't know how to stay so calm in the face of tragedy, even personal tragedy. "The real truth is more complicated than what he's saying."

"More complicated? How could this situation be any more complicated than it is already?"

She sounded pretty subdued herself, deliberately controlled. Slater could guess that she was most likely still thinking about the gun in his hand. He was tempted to pass it over to her right then and say, "See? I'm on your side. I'm one of the good guys, and I'm giving you my gun to prove it." Unfortunately, he couldn't bring himself to do that. He couldn't break one of the first rules he'd learned when he joined the force. A lawman never gives up his weapon, especially not to somebody who is looking at him as if she wished she could freeze him solid with her eyes.

"Believe me. This situation is a lot more complicated than you know," he replied, keeping his voice calm in the hope that she'd stay calm, too.

Slater edged the gun further out of sight behind his body, as if he could get her to be less aware of its presence. He guessed she'd noticed what he was doing, even though she didn't react to it. She was too smart to be thrown off her guard now. They were two cagey characters circling each other, watching every move. He'd been in this position many times before, but on those other occasions he'd never once found himself wishing both of them could end up winning.

"I'm a cop," he said. "A federal investigator working undercover."

There was no way he could tell her that but straight out, at least none he could think of at the moment. He could see the hesitation his words brought to her expression and just a hint of thawing in her eyes. He'd hoped for that, but the instant didn't last. When she spoke, her voice was as cold as it had been before his revelation.

"Prove it," she demanded.

Slater couldn't help but sigh at that, and shake his head a little. He could anticipate what was going to happen and how helpless he'd be to stop it.

"As I said, I'm undercover," he repeated. He could hear his tone of voice reflecting that helplessness already. "I can't carry any official identification. There are people I could have you talk to who would verify who I really am, but that would require a phone call. I don't think we can manage that right now."

This shack barely had furniture in it, much less a telephone.

"A phone call to where?" she asked, still icy and watching like a hawk.

"To Washington, D.C." He could imagine how farfetched that had to sound to her, but he continued anyway. "I work for the Bureau of Alcohol, Tobacco and Firearms. We have good reason to believe Laurent is hooked up with some South American gunrunning interests we've been trying to shut off for years now. My assignment was to get Laurent to trust me so I could infiltrate his organization and find enough proof of his involvement to make charges stick in court and maybe take some of his contacts down along with him."

That was the whole story. It was the truth, but it came across like some cop show plot Slater might have picked up from T.V. He had no proof to back up what he was saying. Only her faith in his word could do that. He could see in her eyes that, if she'd ever had such belief in him, she didn't have it now. He was even more certain of that when she didn't question any of the details of his story further. That told Slater she didn't believe enough of what he'd said to consider it worth questioning.

"What are you planning to do now?" she asked instead.

She was asking that because she was frightened of him. He was almost a hundred percent sure of that. She was just stringing him along now, hoping for a chance to get the upper hand somehow.

"We have to get this man to a hospital," Slater said.

"I don't think he should be moved. One of us will have to go for help."

"I should stay with him," Slater said. "I know quite a bit about gunshot wounds."

"I'll bet you do."

The accusation was in her eyes as well as her words. She was telling him that he knew so much about violence because he was a violent man himself, an outlaw.

"I'm a federal agent," he said. "You have to believe me."

He hadn't meant to plead like that. It just came out. He could feel his position weakening further still with every word he uttered.

"Believe you?" she snapped. "Why would I ever believe you again? Even if this unlikely story of yours happens to be true. Even if you are some kind of policeman or investigator or whatever, that doesn't change the fact that you're a liar. That's the bottom line here, isn't it? Whoever you really are, everything you've ever told me was a lie.''

''Not everything,'' Slater said quietly.

But what truth had he ever told her? Had he ever told her the way he'd come to feel about her? Had he ever murmured that particular truth into her ear, even when they were making love? No, of course he hadn't. He'd been too much the good cop to open up to the suspect even then, especially about anything personal. Now, it was way too late to open up to her about anything. She was too far past being able to hear what would only sound like another one of his lies. Slater felt the gloom of helplessness drop its shroud ever more closely around him.

''Well, if you did tell me anything that happened to be true,'' she replied, ''that doesn't really matter now. All I care about is getting help for my grandfather's friend. I wish I didn't have to trust you to do that, but I have no choice. Otherwise, I'd have to leave you here alone with him and take the chance you might finish off what the others started the minute I was out of earshot.''

Such a direct statement of how little Phoenix thought of him pierced Slater as sharply as the steel that had returned to her eyes could ever have done.

''I'll go then,'' he said.

She caught his arm as he moved to drag his suddenly very heavy bulk up from its crouch next to the still unconscious Blue.

''Why don't you leave the gun with me,'' she suggested, managing a touch of sweetness in her tone. ''I might need it to protect myself.''

Slater couldn't believe her now, either, any more than

she believed him. After all, there'd never been any trust between them before, at least not on his side. She must have figured him for a possible shady character all along. With that kind of history, why should they be able to trust each other now? Besides, rule number one still applied. A cop didn't give up his weapon, not even to the woman he'd tried not to fall in love with but failed.

"You'll be safe till help gets here," he told her.

"What if Sax and Laurent come back?"

"They won't. This is the one place they're sure to stay away from. They know the cops could be on their way by now. Sax and Laurent aren't about to show up anywhere the law might be."

"You know a lot about this sort of thing, don't you?" she jeered. "You know a lot about the way criminals think."

There was the accusing tone again, condemning Slater and his whole way of life, no matter which side of the law he happened to be on.

"Yes, I do," he said. Unfortunately, there was no other answer.

He stood then. He thought about sticking the gun in the back of his waistband so she'd see him as less threatening, but he didn't do that. She might be able to grab the chair next to her and swing on him hard enough to catch him in the legs and bring him down. He could see the wary wiliness of the adversary in her eyes. He had to think of her as that, as his enemy, and act accordingly, however much it sliced his heart apart to do it. He kept his gun out of sight, but he didn't let it go.

"I'll get help," he said.

He turned toward the door. He didn't want to leave her alone here, but he did believe the police were probably on their way right now. That thought quickened

Slater's step toward the door. He couldn't afford the delay that was sure to be involved in explaining himself and proving who he really was.

He was still on the job after all, no matter what he might be going through personally. He'd been assigned to nail Laurent. Now, that was possible. Maybe Slater didn't have what it would take to bring Laurent down on the gun-trafficking charges, but there was attempted murder and conspiracy to commit murder and kidnapping. Slater heard the list of crimes ticking off longer and longer in his head. He had enough on Laurent to put him away for a hundred years, maybe more.

Too bad Slater couldn't manage to feel the least bit good about that now.

"You will send help, won't you?" Phoenix asked as he opened the door. "You won't just leave us here, will you?"

Slater could see the doubt in her eyes. Even when he assured her that medical assistance would be on its way soon, he knew she wouldn't believe him until the ambulance actually arrived.

Too bad Slater couldn't feel good right now about anything at all.

Chapter Twenty

The cliffs were jagged and sparkled along sheer walls with points of shimmering light all the way to their vaulted heights. The blue-black, star-pricked sky above duplicated the scene. The ocean dashed and swirled among the rocks far below with a sound that had a voice in it. "Come to me. Come to me," it crashed and breathed. Phoenix heard the call whispering around her where she balanced on the highest ledge. The wind was sharp at her face and swept her silken gown between her legs and close about her body so that every curve and sinew was displayed for all to see.

She should have been embarrassed by that, especially with the crowd watching as they were from the long, flat lower ledge across the cut between the cliffs. They clamored toward their restraining wall, hungry for a better view. She might have cowered from their impertinent eyes, but she was all boldness now and thrust her breasts high and proud against the satiny smoothness of her sultry gown. She could hear the gasp of appreciation and desire all the way across the chasm. The women wanted to be her. The men wanted to possess her. She tossed her hair back and breathed in the heady perfume of the power that was hers in this moment.

Her toes were bare and decked in rings glittering with precious stones. Rubies, emeralds, sapphires twinkled there as rivals to the stars above and the flashing lights along the cliff side below her feet and the sheer wall opposite. She was the envy of all in earth and heaven. She flexed her bejewelled toes against the rocky edge. Brown-bodied boys perched on lower juttings from the cliff. Their iridescent swimsuits were colored in a hue just lighter than her gown. She could tell that these boys and their taut muscles were waiting for her to move.

She rose, her body straight and purposeful as an arrow, off the cliff and arced for just an instant in the air. Suspended in that flash of time, she saw everything below and around as beautiful and swept clean by the wind and water. She straightened her body then and angled downward from that apex. She was reluctant to leave a vista of such captivating loveliness behind, but she must. Her plunge began, invigorating and free. The rush of wind isolated her in a soft cocoon of breezes as she cut through its resistance. Only herself and nature existed here in this unfettered space between sky and sea. The boys dove around her, their suits gleaming like the gems on her toes. Still, she was alone and drinking in the strength of her solitariness.

Then, everything changed. In an instant as swift and unpredicted as the flip from one page to another, the power and perfume disappeared. There were only rocks below, cold and craggy, beckoning not with the soft voice she'd heard earlier but with cackling, mocking laughter. She was plunging toward them with increasing speed. She tried to flap her arms like wings and soar back up again, but they were plastered to her side by the force of the wind. The boy divers glided on the currents of the wind like gulls, kept safe from the menacing rocks below. The boys smiled sadly but couldn't stop her plunge. Her gown stripped from her then, and the wind turned frigid and piercing against her unprotected flesh.

A gasp went up to heaven from the watchers on the cliffs, and she saw why. Below her on the rocks, a figure had appeared. He was tall and broad. His dark hair billowed in the wind as he lifted his face, all angles and stalwart intention, toward her. His green eyes shone more brightly than the emeralds on her toes. His mind spoke to hers in words that carried on the thought alone. "I will save you," he said without a movement of his lips, and she heard him. He spread his arms open, wide and invincible.

Her heart smiled into his. The fear that had gripped her throat during those moments of terrifying descent toward bare rock evaporated. She was breathing in her first free breath and smiling at him still when he disappeared. She plunged on toward empty, unforgiving, rocky doom as the terror returned, ten times more heart stopping than before. She tried to close her eyes against the harrowing sight, but could not. Her throat opened just far enough to emit a high, thin scream.

Phoenix was still screaming when she awoke just inches from her inevitable impact with a shattering end. She was trembling all over in a shudder that clattered her teeth together. She had kicked the blankets off, maybe at the same moment she lost the silken gown of her dream. She was wet from the intensity and exertion of that downward plummet. Her hair lay plastered against her neck, and the wetness made her shudder more fiercely than ever.

Terror still gripped her heart, which slammed inside her chest and echoed in her ears. Her scream had faded to a whimper which she did her best to quiet as she clamped her teeth tight together against their chattering. She gradually grew sensible enough to understand that all of this shuddering and chattering did not come from her dream. The room she was in happened to be freezing cold. But how could that be? Acapulco was never cold. How many times had her grandfather said that? "Always eighty-five and balmy. It's a wonder they don't die of boredom down there." That had been his little joke, but he always looked melancholy after he made it.

Phoenix awoke fully to the joke of the moment. She was not in Acapulco now. She'd left there some time ago. Was it yesterday or just this morning? She'd flown out at an odd time and couldn't get a direct flight. She remembered slouching in a surreal haze through the Dallas-Fort Worth Airport between connecting flights to New York City. She'd tried to sleep in the airport and on the flights as well, but she couldn't. She'd drifted in that same haze all the way through customs, not truly conscious but also not asleep and definitely not getting any rest.

The cab driver that brought her from JFK International Airport to her Manhattan apartment in the freezing February morning kept glancing at her in the rearview mirror. He was probably wondering if he should drop her off at the Bellevue psych ward instead. She must have looked quite deranged in the rough wool sweater, fake leather shoes and too short slacks she'd bought somewhere—was it on the street in Mexico or at an airport?—to replace the bloodstained ones she'd discarded in some ladies' room trash can.

She'd clutched her beige leather shoulder bag all the way. That bag was an expensive contrast to the rest of her makeshift getup. More important, that bag held very precious contents—her bank and credit cards and, mercifully, her passport as well. That was all she'd rescued from Mexico. Her clothes, her camera, her jewelry, everything else had been left back there in Acapulco, in those perilous hotel rooms where abducting murderers might still lie in wait for her return.

Help had finally come for Citrone Blue at the brickworks shanty near Coyuca. Fortunately, after the police arrived, Blue had revived enough to tell the truth about who had shot him. The police still wanted to hold her for questioning, but let her ride with Citrone to the hospital in Acapulco. In the confusion there, she'd managed to slip out of a side door and away. She remembered now stopping at a vendor across the street from the long, wide flight of steps leading up to the hospital. That was where she'd purchased the odd outfit she was still wearing now and hailed a blue-and-white Volkswagen cab to take her first to a bank machine for cash and then to the airport. All the way, she'd searched the road behind for a black Bronco.

She credited the quickness of her exit, not stopping even to think about what she was doing but heading straight for the airport and away, for her escape. She'd counted on her pursuers not expecting that. They would more than likely underestimate her boldness and resolve. Not even Slater would have guessed how single-minded she could become, like a bullet from one of the vicious firearms they all so routinely carried. She'd headed, true as one of those shots, for home and the purpose she had to fulfill. She'd kept to that course all the way, even through her daze.

That daze and the unreality of her journey north and east had everything to do with pain. Her heart had been split right in two, and the torture of that fatal wound would find no sudden relief. She might have healing in

her future, but that was too far off and abstract to have
any recognizable substance for her now. She could only
carry this heavy ache which threatened to bury her deep
in the darkness of her despair. She mustn't let that happen though, at least not yet. Later on, she might allow
herself to be covered over and sink into grief from the
loss she couldn't allow herself to feel right now. She
might seek that uneasy peace eventually, but not today.
It was evening, the best time to set her plan in motion,
and that was what she had to do.

Phoenix hurried out of bed pulling the blanket along
with her and swaddling herself in it over the sweat-
soaked, mismatched outfit she'd dropped into bed still
wearing however many hours that was ago. The floor-
boards chilled her bare feet. She must have kicked her
shoes off some time in the night—or was it daytime?—
of her uneasy slumber. She switched on radiators and
the space heaters she kept for arctic days in her apartment, which varied in climate during winter from too
much steam heat to drafts that crept out at her from
nowhere.

She hustled into the bathroom, stamping her feet and
hopping up and down to get her blood moving faster
toward the icy extremes of her fingers and fanny. She
was hopping that way when she looked in the mirror
over her bathroom sink. She stopped dead still in shock
at what she saw. No wonder the taxi driver had watched
her so closely. She was amazed he'd let her in his cab
at all. Her dark blond hair was matted and wild from
more than just sleep. Deep, purple circles ringed her
eyes. Their usually clear blue had turned to muddy gray.
Remnants of Mexican dust smudged her forehead and
caught in the creases of her neck. She recognized a particularly knotted place in her matted hair as the caking

of dried blood. Her reddish brown tropical tan had taken on an ashen tinge, as if beneath it there lay the pallor of a ghost's complexion.

Phoenix turned abruptly from the image and lunged for the tub. She twisted the faucets to their familiar positions of just the right temperature for her shower. She turned the hot water faucet up two notches higher still. She needed that extra heat to thaw her out, though she expected to carry this frosty chill at the center of her heart for some time to come.

She hurried out of her clothes as the shower splashed and began to steam. She recognized how rapidly she'd been moving ever since the pall of her dream had subsided enough to let her move at all. She also understood the reason for all of this dashing around. She was trying to widen the distance between herself and that very same dream. Nonetheless, as she stepped into the shower, one stark moment remained vivid before her, as if emblazoned on her eyes for all time—Slater broad as a tree with branches spread and birds singing promises of her salvation, then gone like the puff of empty air he had turned out to be.

SLATER HAD CALLED the police and ambulance from the first phone he found in Coyuca. He'd called back again to make certain they were both on their way, and once more to find out that Phoenix and Citrone Blue had been picked up from the brickworks and were safely on their way to Acapulco and the hospital there. Slater drove the Jeep back down Highway 200 to the city then. The trail after Sax and Laurent was as cold as cold could be by now. They'd probably have watchdogs at each of the three hotels Phoenix and Slater had frequented. He could simply go back to any of those and wait for one of the two creeps, most likely Sax, to pay a visit or follow Slater wherever he might go. That would give Laurent the choice of when and where to make a move, putting Slater at a distinct disadvantage. He wasn't about to let that happen.

Instead, he found a neutral outpost in the lobby of a modest hotel along the Costera on the opposite side from the beach. He staked out the pay phone there and began placing calls to D.C. He had an idea that Phoenix would return to New York, but he couldn't be absolutely sure. He had his D.C. computer mole keep close watch on all of the airlines out of Acapulco airport just in case.

In the meantime, Slater had no clue where she might be. He knew she was smart enough not to go back to any of the hotel rooms they had stayed in. They'd spoken of the impossibility of that on their way to Coyuca. She had access to cash and credit by way of the cards she had with her. He wasn't surprised, though, to find she'd retrieved her passport from the hotel safe at La Escarpadura. She had mobility, and she was smart. Unfortunately, he had a hunch that she was also carrying a stubborn determination to clear any taint of doubt there might be against her name. She'd said something about that back in that shack after Citrone Blue let the cat out of the bag about why so many people had followed her to Mexico.

Slater didn't like to think about cats out of bags. His emerging feline had let forth the most earsplitting shriek of them all. That revelation ripped through whatever connection Slater and Phoenix had like a stiletto slitting through gauze. What they'd had together was just that delicate, too. They hadn't been with each other long enough to build anything more sturdy or resilient. Besides, just as she said, his end of their connection had been built on a pack of lies, a house of cards which toppled at the first breath of truth.

He'd waited in that hotel lobby for hours, with sojourns into the bar every now and then where he had to resist with all his might the temptation to drown his sorrows in *tequila*. As usual, the locals minded their own business. If they thought it was odd for this scruffy, rather wild-eyed *gringo* to be hanging around for most of the afternoon and into the evening, they never questioned him once. He had no doubt they kept a watch on him all the same. From what he'd seen of the Mexican people in these past few days, they might be discreet, but they definitely weren't stupid.

The crucial callback came just in time. The long hours that make up the night for heartsore saps like he'd become were rapidly descending. He wasn't sure how much longer he could resist the siren call of those Cuervo Especial Gold bottles over the bar. He might at least find some respite from the thudding ache in his left shoulder which had reasserted itself, probably because of these hours of inactivity. He was almost ready to order a *tequila* on the rocks or maybe even straight up when the call came. Phoenix had hopped a flight to New York City with a layover at Dallas-Fort Worth, and she was on her way. Slater breathed a sigh of relief to hear that, first because she was out of this town that had become so dangerous for her, and second because he could now get a move on at last himself.

His contacts in high places managed better flight connections for Slater than the ones Phoenix had to contend with. He'd arrived at JFK in New York only a couple of hours after she did. He thought about renting a car then, but he'd had enough of that back in Mexico. Public transport tended to be more efficient in Manhattan anyway. Thinking about that reminded him of all those loose ends he and Phoenix had left hanging around Acapulco and vicinity. One more phone call to Washington assured Slater that the hotel bills would be paid and the various vehicles accounted for. There would even be someone at each of those hotels to collect their belongings and ship them back to the states ASAP.

Slater took a taxi to yet another hotel room, in midtown Manhattan this time. This wasn't the hotel Laurent and Sax knew about, of course. That one was in a much seedier part of town befitting Slater's cover story as the impoverished victim of his gambling ways. Instead, he'd cabbed it to an official hideaway high up inside a tower of steel and glass. A change of clothes appropriate to the bone-chilling season awaited him there. He turned his hot shower to cold when he felt his weariness about to overcome him. He'd slept on the plane, but he was tired still. The king-size bed invited him as temptingly as the *tequila* had done all those hours and the breadth of a continent ago, but once again he wouldn't let himself give in.

That was how he'd come to be here now, shivering in this doorway across from Phoenix's apartment building. A rental car might have been the smart choice after all. At least then he could sit inside somewhere for this stakeout. He'd spent a few hours in the diner on the corner, seated in the window with a clear view of Phoenix's front entry. He'd carried on a mild flirtation with the waitress so she'd let him sit there nursing cup after cup of coffee for that long a time. Then her shift had ended, and he felt it was time to leave. This was New York not Mexico, after all. People could be anything but discreet here, and they didn't care if they stuck their noses in your business, either. The next waitress might not be so accommodating.

Darkness had fallen, and an even deeper chill of the air came with it. Slater was almost ready to call his magic D.C. number and have them send him an automobile for shelter. Then Phoenix emerged from her apartment building across the wide avenue from him, and Slater was suddenly as warm as Acapulco once more.

Chapter Twenty-One

Phoenix did have a plan, and it might even be a good
one. Then again, it might not. Success depended on there
being no glitches. After her experiences in Acapulco, she
wasn't sure it was possible for anything in life to be
glitch-free for her any longer. She tried to stay positive
all the same, even when the chill of February knifed
through her layers of clothing to remind her how her
blood had thinned in just a few weeks of tropical
weather. She did her best not to think about how much
she would prefer to be watching the lights on Acapulco
Bay with a day of lounging at Caleta Beach ahead of
her. Instead, she was trudging through Midtown with her
head tucked into her collar against the wind.

She was also about to do something illegal, but that
seemed to be her stock-in-trade lately. She wasn't sure
if she'd actually broken the law in Mexico. She'd definitely bent it some. Of course, Slater had tried to tell her
he *was* the law. She'd even considered the possibility,
until she had to admit what an exercise in grabbing at
straws that was. She was forever remarking to herself on
how foolish women could be, even very intelligent
women. They could make themselves believe anything,
including an utterly ridiculous story, as long as it was

told by an attractive man. Phoenix wasn't going to let herself do that now, but she certainly did want to.

Meanwhile, she had to concentrate on not getting caught at her current lawbreaking. She'd taken a subway from her upper East Side apartment to Midtown. She usually didn't do that after dark. Traveling around nighttime Manhattan was much safer when accomplished from the back seat of a cab. Unfortunately, taxi drivers keep records. Tonight, that was a greater risk for Phoenix than whatever denizens of the street she might encounter. Besides, she was on Fifth Avenue with people walking up and down, even at this hour. That gave her another reason to keep her face in her collar. She didn't want to be noticed in case one of these passersby might be asked to identify her later. How they would do that she couldn't imagine. She had so many layers of clothes on that she'd added the appearance of many extra pounds, and with her hair tucked inside a wool beret she was virtually unrecognizable. Besides, these were not casual strollers she was encountering. They were hustling along, probably as eager to get out of the cold as she was. Still, she kept her head bent low and her shoulders slouched forward so she'd look not only fatter but shorter as well.

She'd left the subway a full stop away from the one most convenient to Beldon Laurent's office. That was another evasive maneuver to avoid detection. It was also the reason she had so far to walk in the cold. By the time she reached Laurent's building, that walk had been upgraded nearly to a jog. She was freezing, but she didn't hurry into the lobby immediately. Instead, she stopped to compose herself for a moment. She had to get past the night security man who sat at the desk in the lobby between the revolving, polished brass doors onto the street and the elevators that led upstairs. That was going to be tricky. She still had the ID card Laurent had given her but she would have to sign the visitor log and be seen by the guard.

Phoenix was counting on her muffled appearance to pose an identification problem later, if that situation should arise. She would say her ID card and keys were missing, probably stolen or that she'd left them on her desk before her final exit from Laurent's office and his employ. Anybody could have picked them up and used them, including that person in the bulky jacket and beret who showed up here tonight. She planned to sign her name in the log in handwriting not recognizable as her own. Nonetheless, luck would have to be on her side to pull all of this off. She took a deep breath before pushing through the revolving door. She nearly gasped then to discover that a stroke of the luck she so desperately needed was actually hers.

The security guard's post was empty. The log book lay there opened on top of his desk, but he was nowhere in sight. She scanned the cavernous foyer to make certain the guard wasn't lurking behind a column or potted fern. The place was deserted. He must have been called to one of the offices or maybe he was in the men's room. Whatever had caused him to leave his lobby station, Phoenix thanked heaven for it.

She hurried to the elevator bank that served the block of floors including the forty-fourth. The guard could reappear at any second, and her stroke of good fortune would turn to bad luck then and there. She pulled her keys from the pocket of her parka and located the one for the elevator. She'd punched the up button already. She could feel her breath high in her throat and taste her own fear. She was breaking and entering, and she wasn't comfortable doing that at all. She could still back out. All she had to do was turn around right now, run out of this building and not come back. Why was it her job to put the finger on Beldon Laurent? Why was she doing this anyway?

Phoenix did have an answer to that. She was doing her best to make sure Laurent got put behind bars because, if she didn't accomplish that, he'd be free to come after her again just as he had in Mexico. He'd managed to find her there. He could probably do the same wherever she might run to. She couldn't count on the police for protection, either. She'd heard of too many cases where that didn't work—which made her think of Slater again for some reason and his story about being on the official side of the law. If he could make up a whopper like that, maybe he had also fabricated the part about Laurent's alleged Latin American connections and what Phoenix had supposedly come close to uncovering in his files. Her whole plan for tonight depended on that being true, but she had no proof it was, other than Slater's word. Maybe this was yet another exercise in denial, her believing anything he said could be anything but a lie.

Once more, she told herself she could still back out and make a run for it. She shouldn't put her faith in a man who had so thoroughly demonstrated his capacity for deception. On the other hand, what was her alternative? Slater's scenario was the only lead she had to what might have happened to set Laurent so viciously on her trail. She could take a chance that Slater might have been telling the truth for once, or she could go back to her apartment and wait for Sax or somebody like him to show up and end her life. She could also run back to Mexico, or maybe to Europe, and deliberately lose herself this time. For some reason, that was the least attractive possibility of all. When an elevator door opened along the bank in front of her, she hurried into the car, turned her key in the lock, and waited as the doors slid shut again. She pushed the button for the forty-fourth floor, and her fate was sealed.

LUCKILY FOR SLATER, Phoenix hadn't yet put her hat on when she came out of her apartment building. Otherwise, he might not have recognized her. She had on what looked like a jacket she must have borrowed from somebody at least five sizes larger than she was. He supposed that was camouflage, and if he hadn't been watching her entryway at exactly the moment she came out, he might have been fooled. His heart skipped a beat at the thought of that possibility. The last thing he could let happen was to have Phoenix running around this town on her own right now. There was no telling what might become of her then. As it was, he did recognize her, and she did take the subway. These were both happy occurrences as far as Slater was concerned. Subways are easier for hanging on to a tail. Taxicabs can get snarled up in traffic. Slater couldn't afford that tonight.

He'd followed her out of the subway at Central Park South and then onto Fifth Avenue. The fact that she'd taken that subway exit threw him off at first. He'd had a hunch she would head for Beldon Laurent's office. Then she got off the train blocks and blocks away. Nonetheless, Laurent's building was where she ended up. Slater breezed through the lobby after her, thanks to lax security. He took the service stairs up a few flights where he'd guessed right that the elevators wouldn't be locked from the hallway side. He elevatored to the forty-second floor then and returned to the stairs for the rest of the trip. Phoenix was outside Laurent's office with a key in her hand when Slater came up behind her. This was as far as he could let her go on her own.

"Fancy meeting you here," he said.

She swung on him then, leading with the fist that held her keys. If he hadn't been trained to block shots like this one, she'd have tagged him for sure, probably taken him out long enough for her to get away. He caught her arm just before her fist could connect with his nose.

"I know you won't believe this, but I'm here to help."

He'd kept his voice at a whisper, and when she opened her mouth to answer he put his finger to his lips.

"We don't want anybody to hear us," he whispered. "Let's just get out of this hallway. We can argue about what is or isn't true later on."

She hesitated for a moment, staring at him with a look he wished he could erase from her eyes. Then, she sighed and turned back toward the office. In less that two minutes more, they were inside and closing the door to Laurent's reception area behind them. Slater knew immediately that something was wrong. There were lights on farther into the suite. He glanced down the hall and noticed a circle of illumination on the richly designed Persian carpet outside one of the offices. He believed it to be Laurent's office, but that alone wouldn't spell trouble. Lights are left on sometimes in buildings like this one at night. What did concern Slater was the music. Someone was playing what sounded like opera, not very loudly but definitely there. Slater guessed that was coming from the same office with the lights on. Phoenix had already backed off against the wall behind the receptionist's desk. Slater did the same.

"Who do you think it is?" he asked. "Maybe Laurent's back in town. We made it. He could have, too."

Phoenix shook her head emphatically. "It's not Laurent."

"How do you know?"

They continued to whisper even quieter than the level of the low-decibel music.

"Laurent loves opera. He plays it very loud, especially this one. *Aida,* is one of his favorites."

Slater nodded. He wasn't up on his culture enough to know if she was right or wrong about which opera he heard lilting from down the hall. He'd have to take her word for that. As for Laurent's habits, she'd worked for him. Maybe Slater should take her word there, too.

"I wonder who it is, then," Slater mused mostly to himself.

"Let's find out."

Before he could stop her, Phoenix had slipped around the corner from the reception area into the hallway and was already headed toward Laurent's office. Slater would have called out for her to stop or at least to wait, but he didn't want to be heard. Besides, she probably wouldn't listen anyway. Slater slipped along the hallway wall behind her, glad that this time he was carrying a weapon. He'd picked it up at the agency apartment where he'd changed his clothes. He pulled the 9 mm semiautomatic from his back waistband. He kept the gun next to his leg with the barrel toward the floor. If he raised it higher Phoenix could turn around and see it pointed in her general direction and react audibly. He didn't want to risk that now, especially since he had no idea who the music lover in the office just ahead might be.

Slater's peripheral vision registered a number of plaques along the walls to Laurent's office. They hadn't been there when Slater was here before. He glanced closely enough to see that they were in recognition of various acts of public service, big donations probably. Slater was tempted to laugh out loud at the prospect of Beldon Laurent, the philanthropist. This had to be the result of Phoenix's handiwork. Slater could tell from this wall display that she'd done her job well. Laurent would have no trouble coming across as totally legitimate now. He could probably even make the Mexico charges go away. Who was going to take the word of Citrone Blue in the face of the kind of top-notch legal muscle Laurent would have on his side? The rest was Sax's doing, with no absolutely verifiable connection to Laurent. Sax had probably continued on to parts even farther south than Mexico by now anyway. He'd be too hot for Laurent to keep around. In the meantime, there'd be no lack of hoodlum types to take his place. Maybe this was one of them, only a few yards away in the office.

Slater caught Phoenix by the arm. When she looked back toward him, he carefully indicated the gun in his hand and motioned for her to let him go ahead. He was pleasantly surprised when she nodded her head for him to do so. Maybe she really did want company on this caper after all. They executed an under-over maneuver as he slid past her while she sidled into his former position, and they managed that without making a sound. Slater crouched down slowly, close as he could get to the floor. He hoped the creaking in his joints, still stiff and resistant from his physical trials in Mexico, wasn't loud enough for anybody but himself to hear.

He was low enough to risk a peek around the edge of the door frame as long as he was very cautious about it. What he saw made him want to laugh, so much so that he almost did. Maybe that was a desire for tension release here. Having Phoenix in this situation was making him a lot less cool than he liked to be. With that in mind, he motioned for her to move back to the reception area. He straightened partway out of his crouch and followed. Otherwise, she'd have been down this hall like a shot after him again. He was certain of it. Neither of them spoke until they were out of earshot behind the reception area wall again.

"What's going on?" Phoenix whispered.

"It's the security guard."

Once more, Slater had to muffle the urge to laugh.

"What?"

"The night man from downstairs," Slater said. "He's in there leaned back in that big chair with his feet up on Laurent's pink marble desk, smoking one of his cigars and sampling his single malt Scotch."

Phoenix looked disbelieving. "You're kidding me," she said.

Slater couldn't remember whether to hold up two fingers or three, so he just whispered, "Scout's honor."

Merriment danced into Phoenix's eyes, and she clamped her hand over her mouth obviously to keep her own laughter from spilling forth. Something about that moment made Slater even more deeply aware of how very much he didn't want to lose her.

"We have to get rid of him," Phoenix said when she'd composed herself.

Slater nodded. "Any ideas?"

Phoenix was still for a moment. Then she stepped quickly over to the receptionist's desk, studied the phone console for a moment and pushed a couple of buttons. The responding ring in Laurent's office was immediate. At that instant, Phoenix gestured toward the wide space under the reception desk, another example of Laurent's apparent taste for massive office furniture. Phoenix was already scrambling into that cavern. Slater took a few seconds longer to fold his considerable size even into this fairly spacious hiding place. The desk had a solid front and was angled so that anybody passing straight from the inner office hallway to the door of the suite wouldn't be able to see even two people tucked away here. The opera music had come to an abrupt halt as the phone in Laurent's office went on ringing. The sound of that incessant jingle did the trick. Slater heard the security guard hurry past, exit through the suite door and close it behind him. Phoenix ducked out from under the desk and pushed a button on the phone console to stop the ringing, then crouched back down next to Slater. Everything was quiet now, while Slater wished he could simply take Phoenix in his arms and get her out of here instead of pressing on to whatever came next.

Chapter Twenty-Two

Phoenix found what she was looking for right where she'd left it, behind a cabinet in the office that had been hers during her time with Laurent. She'd put this file here on purpose, in case he decided to clean house. She hadn't exactly planned to come back here and face Laurent with what she'd found, but she hadn't exactly planned not to, either. She'd been halfway to Acapulco when she remembered seeing Laurent's private secretary pass by the open door to his office while Phoenix was researching his personal files. That had to be where he assumed she'd come across incriminating information about him.

She'd been doing research into his background during her last day on the job for him. She'd been given carte blanche to check out his files and assumed that included the cabinet in his office. What she found there turned her off wanting to work even one day longer for Beldon Laurent. She hadn't noticed anything overtly criminal, but she'd only given the file a quick once-over before stashing it behind the cabinet in her office and leaving for good. There was no telling what a more thorough examination of this folder might produce, not to mention an in-depth perusal of the rest of the office space, Laurent's pink-and-beige inner sanctum included.

Phoenix began studying the contents of the folder, more carefully this time than she had on her last day working for Laurent. She'd seen the photographs then, with recognizable mob characters and Laurent hanging out together cozy as could be. There were even personal notes attached to some of the shots. That had been enough for Phoenix to figure out he was keeping the kind of company she didn't care to associate herself with even remotely. Still, Slater was the one who could not only identify Laurent's companions but also understand the significance of the dates on the backs of the photographs and the places they'd been taken.

"This is just what we've been looking for," Slater exclaimed. "This puts Laurent right where we want him. On the hot seat. When these other hoods find out what we've got here, they'll be singing like birds to save their own hides before you can say federal indictment."

Meanwhile, Phoenix was shedding yet another layer of apparel. She'd pulled off her beret in the outer office and stuffed it into the pocket of her voluminous jacket. Now it was time to get rid of the jacket as well, before the heating system reduced her to a puddle on the office floor. She was pulling apart the last Velcro front closing when Slater called her over to the desk where he'd laid out the contents of the file she'd stashed away.

"Take a look at this," he said.

Phoenix needed a few more seconds to shed her jacket before joining him. The heat had waved her usually straightish hair around her face and warmed her cheeks to what she knew had to be a bright flush. Slater turned to look at her and stopped still with a sheaf of photographs apparently forgotten in his hand.

"You are so very beautiful," he said in a deep, tremulous voice that thrilled directly to her heart.

Phoenix ducked her head in response, certain that her own sudden tremulousness must show in her eyes. She didn't want him to see that, or she didn't think she wanted him to see it.

"What did you find?" she asked to cover her confusion.

She indicated the file he was holding. Slater glanced back at the folder as if surprised to find it still in his hand.

"This one picture really delivers the goods," he said. "This is a café in Bogotá." He pointed to the obviously Latin American scene. "I've been there, specifically to investigate the people he's sitting with in this shot."

Phoenix examined the photo Slater indicated. None of it meant anything to her.

"Why would Laurent think that my seeing this could put him in jeopardy?" she asked.

"Maybe he's overly suspicious. That happens a lot of times with people who have things to hide. Or, maybe there's more in his files than just these pictures that could hook him up with specific crimes. What matters is that these photos give us justification for a search warrant into his files."

"Shouldn't you have had a warrant to see these in the first place?"

"We'll find a way around that."

"Who are the 'we' you're referring to?"

"Myself and the people I work for. I can say that you, as an employee, invited me here. Or that you found the photos yourself and brought them to me," he said.

"But I'm not an employee here any longer."

"Don't worry. Our legal people will work something out."

"I'm sure you will," Phoenix said.

She couldn't help the annoyance she was feeling. Getting around the narrow and true way of doing things was obviously not new territory for Slater. He did it all the time. He'd done it with her. He even did it for a living. She'd never had much respect for the end justifying the means. She found herself thinking that, if she and Slater were going to be together, he'd have to work on changing some of his ways. She stopped herself in midthought. Whatever gave her the idea that she and Slater would be together in the first place?

"Let's get out of here," she said. She could hear how exasperated she sounded. "You've got what you need."

She turned on her heel then, grabbing her jacket from the chair where she'd left it, and headed for the door out of the room. She heard Slater shut the file drawer and hurry after her, but she didn't look back. She was angry, and the fact that she wasn't exactly sure why made her angrier still. Maybe that anger was what kept her from being more cautious. Maybe that anger was the reason she yanked open the exit door from the reception foyer without thinking and without noticing that Beldon Laurent and SideMan Sax were behind the beveled glass on the other side.

SHE'D CHARGED AT the door before Slater could stop her. It was never a good idea to move into new territory that fast. The thought made him look toward the door just as Phoenix reached it. The two figures beyond the thick, pebbly glass were distorted but definitely there.

"Phoenix, stop," Slater called out, trying to keep his

voice low enough so that only she could hear it. "Don't open the door."

Whether he'd been heard or not was, unfortunately, irrelevant. She'd already turned the knob and pulled. She stood staring at the two men in the doorway. Sax was wearing his usual sneer, and he had a gun in his hand. Slater had also pulled the Beretta from his waistband, but Sax was pointing his weapon directly at Phoenix's heart.

"Drop it," he said with a smirk toward Slater. "You know what I'll do if you don't."

Slater knew all right, and he had no doubt that Sax would follow through on his promise. Slater lowered his weapon to the floor.

"That's more like it," Sax sneered as he and Laurent stepped into the office and Laurent closed the door behind them. "I got the drop on you and your girlfriend for good this time. There ain't going to be any of your damned Mex buddies coming along to save you, either."

"Please, please," said Laurent in his usual oily tone. "I dislike ethnic references. They are completely out of character with the public-spirited person I've become. I must not have my associates besmirching the image Ms. Farraday has so brilliantly concocted for me."

Slater saw Phoenix flinch at that. She'd backed into the office still clutching her jacket. She was looking more distressed by the moment. Slater hoped she could keep her head together long enough to help out if he found an opening to take Sax down. Maybe she could grab something from the desk and throw it. Slater decided it would be good to keep Laurent talking. Maybe that would give Phoenix time to compose herself. She had to get out of range of Sax's gun at least before Slater could make a move.

"I'm surprised you still have Sax here as an associate," Slater said to Laurent. "I would have thought you'd leave him in Mexico. He's going to be pretty hot for you to handle before long."

"Why do you say that?" Laurent asked pulling off his kidskin gloves to reveal the pinky ring flashing on his finger.

"Let's just say that a little birdie told me," Slater answered. "A little birdie from down Washington D.C. way."

"He's a Fed!" Sax snapped. "I told you I had a feeling this guy was a plant all along."

Sax gestured his gun barrel toward Slater, who tensed to attack, then hesitated. Phoenix was still in easy range of Sax's gun. Before Slater could decide whether to risk it or not, she let out a howl that startled even him.

"Oh, no. This is all my fault," she wailed. "What will I do? What will I do?"

Great, Slater thought. *She's losing it. Or, is she?*

A flashing glint in Phoenix's eye told Slater she was faking. She was creating a distraction. And, it worked. For an instant, Sax and Laurent looked just confused enough for Slater to know his moment had arrived. He ducked to the floor in a lightning movement then arced up again fast. He was on a collision course toward Sax. Out of the corner of his eye, Slater saw Phoenix lift that monster down jacket of hers and fling it over Laurent. She was around Laurent in a streak, wrapping him tight in the huge garment so that even his head was covered. She had it on him back to front and was busily securing the Velcro strips behind him like a straitjacket. Laurent's muffled cries could barely be heard through all of that goose down.

In the same moment as Phoenix's leap, Slater's fist

connected with Sax's wrist, and his gun went flying across the room. Sax yelped and grabbed his wrist. Slater could get a grip on both of Sax's hands at once that way. Slater doubled his free hand into a fist, and he swung with more force than he'd ever used against anybody in his life. The muscles in his surf-ravaged shoulder screamed in renewed agony, but he didn't let himself pay attention to that. The sensation of his punch striking Sax's jaw was worth the cost.

Sax groaned and dropped to the floor as Slater scrambled first for Sax's gun and then for his own Beretta. He frisked Sax's motionless body for a backup piece but found only a knife in his boot. He was still out cold.

"This guy's got a glass jaw as shiny as his suits," Slater said.

"This one's all wrapped up, too," Phoenix added with a smile Slater was really glad to see again at last.

Laurent had fallen to the floor, or maybe she'd pushed him down there. Slater had been too busy with Sax to notice. Laurent was flopping around and emitting strangled whoops from inside the jacket that appeared to swaddle him more tightly with every squirm. Slater couldn't help wondering what New York society would think of Beldon Laurent if they could see him now.

PHOENIX HAD ONE MORE visit to make to Beldon Laurent's office, and one more thing to do before she left the image enhancement business entirely behind. Two days had passed since she and Slater took on Laurent and his hired thug. She'd spent most of that time doing her best to convince herself it was good that she'd probably never see Slater again because they obviously came from opposite corners of the universe, too far apart to be reconciled. Besides, she'd been a job assignment to him, nothing more, nothing less. Whatever intimacy had grown between them was just one of those passing things for him. Otherwise, he'd have been in touch with her by now, and she hadn't heard a word from Slater McCain since the last time she saw him, here in this same hallway leading to Laurent's former domain.

Phoenix sighed as she saw that the crime scene tape was still in place across Laurent's threshold and a federally issued padlock was on the door. Phoenix's key wasn't going to work after all. Another hassle to contend with, as if she wasn't already feeling discouraged enough. She sighed again and stuffed the key back into her purse. She'd have to go through a mountain of red tape to get back inside here. She hoped her downcast spirit would allow her enough energy to get through all of that.

"Let me be of assistance."

The voice she'd heard in her thoughts and dreams for almost forty-eight hours sounded even more wonderful, and even more devastating, in person. Phoenix whirled around and unintentionally caught Slater in the elbow. He moaned, and that was when she saw that his arm was in a sling.

"I'm so sorry," she said before she could think to act cool and distant like she'd told herself she would if and when she ever did happen to encounter him again.

"I'll live," he said, though he did look pained.

"What are you doing here? I thought your part of this investigation was finished."

"Let's just say I've been keeping an eye on you."

"You've been following me?"

"It's one of the things I do best, you know," he said.

As so often seemed to happen when she was with him, Phoenix wasn't certain whether to be flattered or angry.

"I had to know what you'd do next," he said, more softly than was usual for him. "And, maybe I had to think about what I should do next, too."

"So you put me under surveillance?"

"Yes, I did, and I don't think I've ever been on the trail of a more solid citizen in my entire career."

"I suppose I should be glad to hear that, but I'm not accustomed to having my privacy invaded. At least, I wasn't till I met you."

"Well, you should be glad I did it this time," he said with an exasperating, though undeniably attractive twinkle in his eye. "If I hadn't, I wouldn't be here now with this." He dangled a key in front of her. "A little leftover from the investigation."

She guessed he was referring to the police padlock on Laurent's office door. She reached for the key. In that instant, his one good arm swept around her, and his lips were on hers. Somewhere in the timeless space of a long, deep kiss, Phoenix forgot all about being cool and distant and all about the universe of difference that separated them in so many ways. All she could remember was that, somewhere between a hot night in Acapulco and this frigid afternoon in Manhattan, she had fallen in love.

"I guess I could use your services for changing my image some," Slater said when they finally could breathe well enough to speak again and had let themselves into Laurent's former office.

"What did you have in mind?"

Phoenix was collecting the plaques from the hallway wall. She would contact every one of these organizations with the real facts about Beldon Laurent and her own apology, too.

"Something on the order of making me into the kind

of man who knows the truth from the lies for sure
again.''

Slater's green eyes told the truth of what he was feeling right now. Phoenix was certain of that.

"You may have to stay above ground for a while to
make that happen," she said.

"I'm ready for the light of day as long as it's shining
on the two of us together."

"It's a deal," she said. "You'll be my final client."

"I have to warn you I'm a tough case. I anticipate
that this will be a lifetime project for you."

Phoenix smiled up at him. "I know," she said, and
they kissed again.

The three McCullar brothers once stood strong against the lawlessness on their ranches. Then the events of one fateful night shattered their bond and sent them far from home. But their hearts remained with the ranch—and the women—they left behind. And now all three are coming

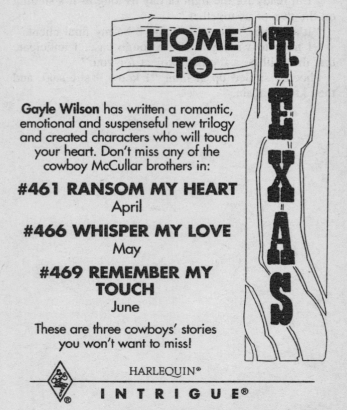

HOME TO TEXAS

Gayle Wilson has written a romantic, emotional and suspenseful new trilogy and created characters who will touch your heart. Don't miss any of the cowboy McCullar brothers in:

#461 RANSOM MY HEART
April

#466 WHISPER MY LOVE
May

#469 REMEMBER MY TOUCH
June

These are three cowboys' stories you won't want to miss!

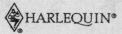

HARLEQUIN®

Not The Same Old Story!

 Exciting, glamorous romance stories that take readers around the world.

 Sparkling, fresh and tender love stories that bring you pure romance.

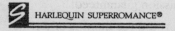 Bold and adventurous—Temptation is strong women, bad boys, great sex!

 Provocative and realistic stories that celebrate life and love.

Contemporary fairy tales—where anything is possible and where dreams come true.

 Heart-stopping, suspenseful adventures that combine the best of romance and mystery.

Humorous and romantic stories that capture the lighter side of love.

Look us up on-line at: http://www.romance.net   HGENERIC

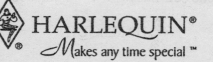

DEBBIE MACOMBER

invites you to the

HEART OF TEXAS

Join Debbie Macomber as she brings you the lives and loves of the folks in the ranching community of Promise, Texas.

If you loved Midnight Sons—don't miss Heart of Texas! A brand-new six-book series from Debbie Macomber.

Available in February 1998 at your favorite retail store.

Heart of Texas by Debbie Macomber

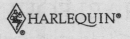

HARLEQUIN®

HPHRT1